The fire that had been smoldering between them flamed to life.

She kissed him, pressing into him, yielding to him. Letting go of whatever trouble waited outside the cabin. In the passion of the kiss, it didn't exist. There was only Johnny.

In the rational part of her brain, she knew none of this made sense. She was kissing Johnny Kreel but she didn't trust him. She didn't even know him.

Familiar's meow caught her attention.

"He's trying to tell us something," she said as the cat ran to the back door and clawed at it.

As Stephanie opened the door, she saw it. A hooded figure silhouetted against the dawn sky—holding a lead rope on her prized stallion. As the figure brought a whip down across the horse's back, the stallion reared and bolted.

"Black Jack!" She started out after the stallion, but Johnny's grasp caught and stopped her. He manhandled her back into the relative safety of the cabin. "I've got to—"

"No," he said, cutting her off. "He's got a gun. And you're the one he's aiming for."

Dear Reader,

Twenty-five years ago, I walked into a local bookstore in Ocean Springs, Mississippi. One of the salesclerks knew I loved mysteries, and she pointed out a new line of Harlequin books—one that combined romance and mystery. I was instantly hooked. What could be better? I loved the combination of vivid characters and exciting action so much, I decided to try to write one.

My first Intrigue, *The Deadly Breed,* involved horses. But when I wrote a book about a black cat detective, Familiar, I realized that I'd opened the door to unlimited adventures. Familiar and I are very proud to be a part of this landmark 25th anniversary for Harlequin Intrigue.

Happy reading!

Caroline Burnes

CAROLINE BURNES

FAMILIAR SHOWDOWN

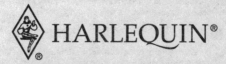

HARLEQUIN®

TORONTO • NEW YORK • LONDON
AMSTERDAM • PARIS • SYDNEY • HAMBURG
STOCKHOLM • ATHENS • TOKYO • MILAN • MADRID
PRAGUE • WARSAW • BUDAPEST • AUCKLAND

For Aleta Boudreaux, who saves and neuters countless cats, making the world a better place for all of us.

Recycling programs
for this product may
not exist in your area.

ISBN-13: 978-0-373-69420-4

FAMILIAR SHOWDOWN

Copyright © 2009 by Carolyn Haines

www.eHarlequin.com

Printed in U.S.A.

ABOUT THE AUTHOR

Caroline Burnes has written fifteen books in her Fear Familiar series. She has her own black cat, Familiar's prototype, E. A. Poe, as well as Miss Vesta, Gumbo, Maggie and Chester. All are strays and all have brought love and joy into her life. An advocate for animal rights, Caroline urges all her readers to spay and neuter their pets. Unchecked reproduction causes pain and suffering for hundreds of thousands of innocent animals.

Books by Caroline Burnes

*Fear Familiar
†The Legend of Blackthorn

CAST OF CHARACTERS

Stephanie Ryan—is following a dream to rescue and train abused horses. Though she'd planned to create Running Horse Ranch in the wild beauty of South Dakota with her fiancé, the untimely death of Rory Sussex has forced her to go it alone. But beyond the borders of the ranch, forces are aligning that she'd never imagine.

Johnny Kreel—knows how to "cowboy up" when it comes to dangerous broncs and flying bullets, but he also has skills not normally found in a cowhand. When he appears at Running Horse Ranch, danger is hot on his heels. Is he there to help Stephanie or merely to weave another web of lies?

Familiar—the black cat detective, finds himself caught in the middle of a complex lie that brings danger to Stephanie and everyone—and everything—close to her.

Rory Sussex—was a charismatic pilot who captured Stephanie's heart and future when he asked her to marry him and build a ranch based on the horse-training principles of Stephanie's Oglala grandfather. When Rory disappeared in a plane crash in the Darien Jungle, he left behind a surprise that pulls Stephanie into danger.

Rupert Casper—is a neighbor of Stephanie's and a man who's used to having his way—no matter what the consequences. When a headstrong stallion injures Casper, the horse ends up in Stephanie's care, and she's determined to protect the horse from Casper's ugly temper. But how far will Casper go to prove his point?

Carlos Diego—is a known criminal, and his harsh hand touches international events on many levels. But why would a man like Diego take an interest in Stephanie and her horse ranch?

Chapter One

October is normally my favorite month. Eleanor, my humanoid, lights the first fire of the season in the library, and I curl up on my favorite green velvet pillow, the one that brings out the color of my eyes. But I'm not in Washington, D.C., where I belong. I'm in South Dakota. At the foot of the Black Hills. On a horse ranch of all things. And these aren't even nice horses. These are rogues and outlaws.

The only benefit is that I get to hang with one fine-looking woman. While I feel Stephanie Ryan wastes a whole lot of energy on those bad horses, I have to admit that she looks good in tight jeans, boots and even those chaps. With her long, straight chestnut hair and those dark eyes, she could be some cowboy's fantasy. And she has a special way with horses. Or at least that's what Eleanor says. She's a "gentler." That's someone who helps troubled horses and makes them safe.

She's out there right now working with that devil horse, Black Jack. He's black sure enough—in color and temperament. In the fifteen minutes I've been watching, he's charged at Stephanie and tried to trample her. All she wants him to do is trot the circumference of the round pen.

And he knows it. Yet he acts like she's trying to kill him. That horse has got a screw loose, and someone is going to get hurt if she isn't careful. If I could vocalize in human language, I'd suggest that she yield the battle and get out of that pen.

Why did Eleanor and Peter leave me here at Running Horse Ranch on the backside of nowhere? They told me to watch out for Stephanie. But who can protect a crazy broad who walks into a small pen with a homicidal equine?

This is going to be a long two weeks. I'm counting the hours until Eleanor returns and takes me back to civilization. It's not that South Dakota isn't spectacular. It is. It's one of the prettiest places I've ever been. And the history here, in the heart of the Sioux nation, is fascinating. But it isn't home. I'm just ready for autumn snuggles with my Clotilde. Ah, the sleek delight of her tricolored calico fur, and the elegant span of her whiskers. They way we spoon together in a sunny window and the way she grooms my face…

Such activities are not to be. I'm here with a raging stallion. Look at that black devil rear. He's spectacular, in a bad boy kind of way. Flaring nostrils, flying mane and— Duck, Stephanie! He's trying to kill her! He's going completely nuts and is trying to strike her with a front hoof.

I've got to do something!

STEPHANIE DODGED THE HOOF by a fraction of an inch. She hit the ground and rolled toward the metal panel of the round pen, but there wasn't enough room for her to slide underneath.

Instinct warned her and she scrabbled to her feet and dove just as Black Jack's two front feet came down exactly where she'd been lying.

Stephanie had to admit that in the two weeks she'd been working with Black Jack, she hadn't overcome his hatred of humans by one iota. Rupert Casper had really done a number on the animal. She didn't want to know the details. She already despised Casper and everything he stood for. Her job was to bring Black Jack around. If she didn't, Casper would most likely kill him.

But right now wasn't the time to worry about the distant future. If she didn't get out of the round pen, she wouldn't have a future at all.

To her utter amazement, she saw the black cat dart between Black Jack's back feet. It provided just enough distraction so she could hurl herself across the round pen. She had to get out. But when she was halfway up the metal panel, she saw the horse close the distance.

Ears flat and teeth bared, he bit her shoulder.

Pain shot through her, but she didn't let go of the metal bars. If she fell under his feet now, he would stomp her to death.

The pain of the bite was so intense that she felt her hands weaken. She'd never seen a horse truly intent on killing a human. She'd heard stories, but hadn't believed them. Something awful had been done to Black Jack, and it was going to take a lot to overcome it—if she lived that long.

Just when she thought she had to let go, the cat leaped onto the horse's back, a move that made the stallion wheel and try to bite the cat. Stephanie heaved herself up the panel.

"Hold on." The stranger came out of nowhere. With one vault, he was in the round pen with her. His arms closed around her hips and he hefted her over the panel and dropped her on the outside.

Before he could get out, the horse turned on him.

Lying in the dirt, heaving to catch her breath, she watched the horse and the man square off. The man made no threatening moves toward the horse, but he didn't run. He held his ground, using the palm of his hand to indicate to the horse that he should come no closer.

To her amazement, Black Jack skidded to a halt. He pawed the ground and snorted. His eyes rolled, showing the whites, and he tossed his mane. While he was dangerous, Stephanie had to admit that he was also beautiful. As was the black cat, who'd come over to her and was licking her cheek with a sandpaper tongue.

"Easy, boy," the stranger said to the horse. His voice was low, almost a whisper. He turned sideways to the horse and the two of them began to walk slowly around the pen, each ignoring the other. To Stephanie, it looked like a choreographed dance, performed by a troupe from some royal academy.

"You okay?" the stranger asked.

"Yeah." She pushed up to a sitting position, her body feeling every thud she'd taken in the last ten minutes.

"You're bleeding." The man continued to pace the small enclosure. He made no attempt to move closer to the horse, but he gave no ground, either.

She looked at her shoulder. He was telling the truth. Blood had soaked through her shirt and was dribbling down her arm. "Doesn't look life-threatening," she said.

"Anybody ever tell you that it was stupid to climb in a pen with twelve hundred pounds of bad attitude?"

"Maybe." She had no intention of explaining her actions to him. His behavior was unusual—she conceded that. But his dress, the worn jeans that hugged his lean body, the dusty boots and the blue chambray shirt that softened his hazel eyes—those things told her he was a cowboy. The one thing she didn't need was a cowboy tending to her business.

"What's this fella's name?" he asked.

"Black Jack."

"He's a fine specimen, but his attitude sucks." In two seconds, the cowboy vaulted out of the pen.

Black Jack stood for a moment as if he were transfixed. Then he charged the panel so hard he shook the entire round pen.

"What did you do to him?" she asked.

"That's exactly the question I wanted to ask you. What the hell did you do to this animal to make him hate you so much?"

Stephanie arched her eyebrows. She wasn't insulted in the least. It was exactly the question she would have asked had she come upon the same scene. "I don't know who you are or where you came from, but that's the right question. And you've got a keen sense of timing." She pushed herself off the ground and stood. Her shoulder was killing her, but she'd never show it. "What's your name?"

"Johnny Kreel."

She held out her hand. "Stephanie Ryan." She looked beyond him toward the barn. Parked beside it was a beat-up truck and horse trailer. She'd been so intent on Black Jack and staying alive that she hadn't heard the cowboy drive up.

Familiar was at the truck and trailer, scoping it out. Eleanor had told her, and insisted it was true, that the cat was some kind of private detective. He did seem inordinately curious about things. Some would even call his brand of curiosity nosiness.

"I've been on the rodeo circuit," Johnny said. "I saw your

barn and wondered if you needed any help. Fence mending, building, things like that. And I can handle horses."

"I can see that." Stephanie considered this stranger. She'd been on the ranch alone for the past four months, and she'd come to realize that the spread was more than she could manage. She'd actually been thinking about a hired hand. "What would you expect for wages?"

Johnny looked around. "Say, for the first two weeks, I'd work for food and lodging for me and Tex." He pointed to the horse trailer. "Tex is my gelding. We've been working the stock at the shows, but Tex hurt his leg and I need a place for him to rest up."

Food and a roof was the best deal Stephanie had heard in a long time. She'd spent everything she had creating Running Horse Ranch. She hadn't expected to carry the burden of starting the horse-training facility by herself, but fate had been harsh. And she was almost out of money.

"It's a deal," she said. "Put Tex in the first stall on the right. His buddy will be Layla, a sweet little mare that gets along with everyone."

Johnny smiled, and Stephanie took a step back. Johnny was a handsome man, a graceful man with the confidence of a rodeo athlete. After what had happened with Rory Sussex, she had no use for any of that in her life.

"Thanks," he said.

"Thank me by getting busy." She was brusque and she knew it. That's the way it was going to be. Johnny Kreel could work at Running Horse for a few weeks, but she had no desire to be his friend or anything else.

"Yes, ma'am," he offered.

She checked his gray-green eyes to see if he was mocking her, but she saw only sincerity. "I need to get

Black Jack into the small barn." She pointed to a stout structure with an eight-foot fence around the paddock area. She'd had it specially constructed for rank horses—until she could bring them around. "There's a lead rope at the round pen gate. He was fine when I brought him out, but…"

"I need to tell you up front, Miss Ryan, that I won't manhandle an animal." He squinted against the sun in his face. "Some folks get upset when they realize I won't cut corners when I'm working with one."

This time Stephanie couldn't stop the smile that she felt spread across her face. "Glad to hear that, Johnny, because I won't tolerate such tactics. My grandfather was a horse gentler. His method has been passed down to me. I've never seen a horse that couldn't be gentled."

Johnny nodded. "Then we'll get along fine. Now I'd best get to my chores. I'll move Black Jack and then go take care of that fence over by the pumphouse. By the time I finish with that, I reckon supper should be ready."

Stephanie stopped short. "That's a good assumption. And pretty accurate, except for one thing. If you want a hot supper, you might get in the kitchen and cook it. I said I'd provide food. I didn't say I'd be your chef." She turned and walked away before Johnny could see the smile tugging at the corners of her mouth. Sometimes it was too much fun to unsettle the gender expectations of a Wild West man.

She'd hardly gone ten steps when she heard the sound of a vehicle. Her driveway sloped around the gentle swells of the land, disappearing from view and then reappearing on the top of the next hill. She put her hand up to shade her eyes as she spotted the black pickup stirring up a cloud of dust as it headed toward her.

"Damn," she said softly.

Johnny examined the approaching vehicle. "Someone you know?"

"The guy who owns Black Jack. Rupert Casper is his name, and he's a real piece of work. His ranch is about two miles as the crow flies, maybe four miles if you take Dry Gulch Road," she said. Johnny didn't say anything, but Stephanie saw the muscle in his jaw jump into play.

"You'd better take care of your shoulder," he said without taking his eyes off the driveway. "I'll explain to Mr. Casper that you're indisposed."

Stephanie shook her head. "I wish it were that easy. Casper's going to want to know how much progress I've made with Black Jack. When he finds out I can't even lead him to his stall, he's liable to shoot him on the spot."

Her words made the muscle in Johnny's jaw bunch even tighter. "We'll see about that."

Stephanie had no use for Rupert Casper, but she put a restraining hand on Johnny's arm. This wasn't a fight he could win. Neither could she. "It's a long story, Johnny. Black Jack is his horse. The horse hurt Casper, and he was going to kill Black Jack but his men brought him over here two weeks ago. I've been dreading this moment."

The pickup stopped not twenty feet from Stephanie. Dust rolled over the top, and a tall man with perfectly trimmed blond hair got out from behind the wheel. His jeans were creased perfection and his boots were polished to a high sheen. The only flaw in his appearance was the white sling that held his left arm. Casper's gaze swept over her bloody shoulder, torn shirt and dust-covered jeans.

"Stephanie," Rupert Casper said as he came forward. He

looked at Johnny but didn't acknowledge him. "How's my horse doing?"

"We're making progress," Stephanie said. She noticed that Familiar had left her side and was sniffing the tires on Rupert's truck like a dog.

"Did Black Jack do that to you?" Casper asked, pointing to her shoulder. He looked past her to the stallion in the round pen. The horse seemed to sense Rupert's attention. He pinned his ears and snaked his head out, striking the metal panel with his teeth.

"I did it to myself," Stephanie said. "Black Jack's a hard case. I won't deny it. But he'll come around."

"He's a danger. I fired the two men who brought him over here. They disobeyed me when I told them to shoot him."

Stephanie could see that Casper took pleasure in his power. "They thought they were doing the right thing. They knew how much money you had invested in the horse."

"It's my money." He walked toward the round pen.

Black Jack spun on his hindquarters.

"He's got a lot of potential," Stephanie said. "If you'll give me more time, I can bring him around, and he'll make a champion cutting horse. He's got the build and the bloodlines."

"He's a rogue. I think the best thing I could do with him is cut my losses and put him in a dog-food can." Casper walked back to his truck, opened the passenger-side door and brought out a rifle. "He's as rank as he was the day he came here. Not even you can work magic on this beast."

He started walking toward the round pen.

"You can't shoot him here." Stephanie looked at Johnny, who was watching the exchange without saying a word.

"I'll send one of the boys with a backhoe to bury him tomorrow."

"Rupert, you misunderstand me. I'm telling you that you can *not* shoot him on my property." She stepped in front of Casper. "I won't allow it."

Casper shifted the gun and a look of astonishment was quickly replaced by anger.

Stephanie noticed that Johnny moved forward so quickly and with such grace that he was beside Rupert Casper in no time. Johnny was a good man to have on her side in a pinch.

"Before you do anything, let me show you the progress we've made with Black Jack," Johnny said softly.

Rupert turned to him as if he'd just become aware of the other man's presence. "Who the hell are you?"

"Johnny Kreel." He didn't hold out his hand, and he didn't say anything else. He went to the round pen, climbed over the panel and walked toward Black Jack without any hesitation.

The stallion blew twice, his eyes rolling for a moment before Johnny caught his halter and snapped on the lead rope that he'd picked up. Without a wasted movement, he opened the gate, led the stallion out and away from Rupert and Stephanie.

"Well, I'll be damned," Casper said. "No one's ever been able to lead that horse."

Though she'd been leading Black Jack for the past two weeks, the horse wasn't reliable. He'd be fine, and then he'd blow up, as he'd done earlier that day. Stephanie was amazed that Johnny had been able to handle him, but she was smart enough to keep it to herself.

"We *are* making progress," she said. "If you don't want

to keep Black Jack, I'll buy him." She'd offered more than once, though she had no idea where she'd get the money to pay for the horse. She'd figure something out.

"He's my horse," Casper said. "If I can't ride him, no one is going to."

That was typical of a man like Rupert Casper. Everything was a possession. It was ego, pride and vanity. "If you'll give me some time, you'll be riding him and taking blue ribbons in the cutting competitions."

Casper stared at the horse until Black Jack disappeared into the barn. "I'll be back in a couple of days. We'll see how much progress you've made."

Stephanie clamped her mouth shut, even though she wanted to shred Rupert Casper with her tongue. Casper was the kind of man who took his anger out on helpless creatures. Black Jack would suffer.

When she turned away from the round pen, she saw the cat jump out the window of Casper's truck. Rupert opened his truck door and swung in.

"Son of a gun!" He jumped out of the truck as if the seats were on fire. To Stephanie's amusement, she saw a dark circle of dampness on the butt of his creased jeans.

"That cat peed in my truck!" Casper's face was scarlet with anger. "I saw that black cat hanging around here. Where is he?" He still held the rifle and he swung around looking for the cat.

Stephanie was loving every second of it. "Are you sure it's cat urine?" She stepped over to the truck and caught the distinctive smell. "Pe-ew! It's cat urine all right." It took all of her restraint not to laugh out loud. And there was no sign of the cat. It was almost as if he knew what he'd done and skedaddled. Eleanor insisted that Familiar was highly intelligent, but Stephanie hadn't believed her. At least not one hundred percent.

"I'll never be able to get that smell out of my truck," Casper said angrily.

"I'm sorry, Rupert. As I told you, I don't have any cats. Maybe it happened somewhere else and you—"

"If I see that black son of a—he's dead."

Stephanie shrugged. "I don't know what to say."

Casper got into the truck and slammed the door as hard as he could. He swung wide and made a U-turn in the middle of her yard. She watched him drive away.

She was still standing there when the cat sauntered out from behind a watering trough. He rubbed against her legs and purred.

"You did that on purpose, didn't you?" she asked, bending to stroke him. There was something special about Familiar, something uncanny.

"Me-ow." He looked up at her and slowly nodded his head.

"Holy cow," she said, kneeling so that she could scratch under his chin. "Eleanor wasn't kidding." She picked him up and kissed him. "And I'm proud of you. But we'd both better stay out of Rupert Casper's way as much as we can."

Chapter Two

Black Jack entered his stall willingly enough and even allowed Johnny to remove his halter. He stood docile and well-mannered until Johnny stepped out of the stall and started to close the door. Then he lunged. But Johnny was ready for him. He'd seen horses like Black Jack before.

And he knew what often happened to them. They paid with their lives for the mistreatment they'd received.

"You've got a chance here, boy," he said softly. "That woman out there wants to help you. Me, too. But the hard work is going to be up to you. If you don't come around…" He hung the halter on a peg outside the stall door and went to get Tex out of the trailer.

He examined the cut on Tex's leg, hosed it down, rewrapped it and put the gelding out to graze in the small paddock that adjoined his stall. All the while he kept glancing toward the ranch house, hoping to see Stephanie headed his way.

From the gossip he'd heard about her in the small town, he'd expected her to be beautiful. As best he could tell, that was one of the many problems she faced. Folks didn't understand a beautiful woman moving out on an isolated ranch alone. It went against the norm and had added fuel to the fire of speculation.

In the two days he'd spent in Custer, South Dakota, before coming out to the ranch, he'd heard all kinds of rumors about her, everything from her practicing black magic to being some kind of felon hiding from the law.

None of that was true. That much he knew for certain. She was a strong woman who'd refused to give up on her dream even after suffering a terrible loss. But folks in town didn't know that. Obviously, Stephanie didn't feel the need to talk about her personal business, and thank goodness for that.

The townsfolk didn't know anything about her past or the hardships she'd been through. But he did. It was her past that had brought him to Running Horse Ranch.

He felt a painful jab in his hamstring and whipped around to find the black cat digging his claws into his legs.

"Hey!" He tried to step away, but the cat stayed with him. "Let go!"

Familiar released his claws and sat down, his gaze steady. Johnny laughed uneasily. It was almost as if the cat had read his thoughts. While he had a healthy respect for the intuitive abilities of all creatures, he didn't believe a cat could read minds. At least he hoped not. Because what he'd come to Custer to do required deception.

While the rodeo story he'd told Stephanie was true, it was a long, long way from the whole truth.

Footsteps thudded in the barn and he latched the door to Tex's paddock, then turned to meet Stephanie. She was a tall, willowy silhouette in the barn door, and he felt again the pounding attraction.

"Is your horse okay?" she asked, walking to the stall door and leaning against it as she appraised Tex.

"He's healing. He hung his leg in a gate."

"Looks like you know your way around a bandage."

Johnny nodded. "You work around stock, you have a lot of opportunities to learn first aid."

"Where have you worked?" she asked.

Her dark gaze settled on him, and he knew she was nobody's fool. He had to be careful, because Stephanie was the kind of woman who checked things out.

"Most recently, I was over in Rapid City. The Big Bar Ranch, Mr. Linton. Before that, I handled the stock at the Missoula rodeo for Gateman Ames. Both of those men will give me a good reference. I didn't have any problems on the job."

She nodded. "I like to know who I'm dealing with."

After what she'd been through, he didn't blame her.

"I'm ready to fix that fence," he said. "Where are your tools?"

"In the shed. Should be everything you need."

"Thanks, ma'am." He felt her gaze as he walked out into the sunshine and on toward the toolshed.

THE STEW MEAT SIMMERED on low heat, and Stephanie raked the carrots into the pot. While she had no intention of becoming a cook for the hired hand, she was also a realist. There wasn't a burger joint or café within fifty miles of Running Horse Ranch. The ranch was nestled in a shallow valley at the foot of the Black Hills. The closest town was a long way off, and cell phone reception and even the satellite for her computer were highly unreliable. If Johnny Kreel was going to eat, someone at Running Horse Ranch was going to have to cook.

While she might get by with a peanut butter sandwich, she couldn't expect Johnny Kreel to go without a decent meal.

She could hear the sound of the skill saw and then the solid thwack of a hammer against a nail as he repaired the fence. He was a fast worker. A hard worker. And she'd spent more time than she should staring out the kitchen window, watching him. A competent man at work was a pleasure to observe. Especially one who looked like Johnny.

He was handsome in a rugged way, and if she'd been in the market for romance, he'd certainly fit the bill—dark-brown hair with a slight curl, hazel eyes that shifted between gray and green, dimples, a hint of a five o'clock shadow. He certainly looked good in his cowboy shirt, and he moved with grace and economy.

The way he'd handled Black Jack intrigued her. Why had the horse responded so quickly to him when she'd worked for the past fourteen days—seemingly in vain—to build trust with the stallion?

That more than anything else captured her imagination. Horses were normally good judges of character. They didn't trust all humans, but Black Jack had trusted Johnny. Could she trust him? That remained to be seen.

While she pondered the mysteries of Johnny Kreel, she chopped the onions and potatoes and added them to the bubbling stew. It wasn't a fancy meal, but it would be filling.

She turned the stove down and picked up her cell phone. Luck was with her—she had reception. Within ten minutes, she'd spoken with Mr. Linton at Big Bar Ranch and Mr. Ames in Missoula. Both gave Johnny high marks as an employee and both said they hated to lose him, but that he'd been a man who kept moving. It was the cowboy way.

She hung up the phone and returned to the window. Johnny had finished the fence and was gathering up the tools. What kept a man on the move? In the days of the old West, it wasn't uncommon for a cowpoke to drift from ranch to ranch, working the seasons of calving, branding and driving to market. But those days were gone.

Even cowboys needed regular pay, a place to live and insurance.

So why was Johnny Kreel on the move?

Maybe she'd never have an answer to that question, but she'd never forget that there was a question. No one was ever going to raise her expectations and send them crashing again.

"Meow."

She looked down to find the black cat at her feet. He head-butted her shin and then looked up at her. "Meow."

"Hungry?"

He did that slow nod again and she had to wonder—for at least the third time—if the cat was actually answering her question.

"Eleanor left some poached salmon for you."

"Meow."

It sounded like the cat said yes. Extraordinary. She got the fish from the refrigerator and prepared a portion for him. When he started eating, she shook her head as she set the table for dinner.

Dusk was falling. The days were short in October, and the nights could be nippy. She'd stocked the bunkhouse with blankets, but she had an extra down comforter.

She went to the back door. "Johnny, dinner's ready!"

Before he appeared, she returned to her work in the kitchen, humming softly to herself as she set the table for two.

GETTING INTO THE RANCH HOUSE was the first step. Johnny didn't feel good about what he meant to do, but he didn't have a choice. Not really. He was accomplished at his job, and that's why he'd been sent to Running Horse Ranch in the first place.

He opened the screen and stepped into the delicious aroma of cooking stew. Despite Stephanie's caustic words, she'd rustled up some grub for him. Against his better judgment, he felt a jolt of pleasure. He quickly reminded himself that he was at the ranch for a purpose, and one that would undoubtedly put him at odds with the horse trainer.

"Have a seat." Stephanie pointed at a stout wooden table. A small cluster of wild prairie flowers in a delicate vase graced the rough-hewn table, and Johnny thought the contrast perfectly symbolized Stephanie. She was as beautiful as the flowers and the fragile vase, and as durable as the old, scarred table.

He stopped his thoughts dead. He could not afford to romanticize Stephanie Ryan. She was part of a mission, part of his job.

"Something wrong?" Stephanie asked as she brought the stew to the table and took her own seat.

"No." He answered too quickly. He lifted the glass of red wine at his place and took a sip. Before he could swallow, something sharp and wicked gripped his shin.

He exploded up from the table, wine flying everywhere.

"What the hell?" he exclaimed.

Both he and Stephanie ducked to look under the table where Familiar sat, placidly licking his paw in total innocence.

Stephanie cleared her throat, leaned over and refilled his wineglass, ignoring the stain all down the front of his shirt.

"That cat is a dangerous beast," Johnny said. He felt like an utter fool. The cat had caught him by surprise.

"That cat is an extraordinary judge of character," Stephanie said, her level brown gaze locking on him. "He peed on Rupert Casper's truck seat."

Johnny didn't believe her at first. It took only a few seconds for him to realize the truth of her statement. "That's pretty incredible." He grinned. "And pretty great. I can forgive him for making me spill the wine if he's going to harass Rupert Casper."

Stephanie held her spoon aloft. "I'm just wondering why Familiar found it necessary to attack you." She left the words hanging between them.

"Maybe he doesn't like the smell of cowboy," Johnny said.

Stephanie took a dainty spoonful of the stew. She swallowed and put down her spoon. "Oh, I don't think Familiar objects to the smell of cowboy, but I'm certain he has a keen dislike of the smell of a rat."

Johnny froze. For one split second, he wondered how Stephanie had unmasked his cover so quickly, but then he realized she'd merely taken a stab in the dark. He forced a chuckle. "Oh, then I'm safe." But he wasn't. Not if Stephanie found out what he was really up to.

He bent over the bowl and began to eat. While it wasn't fancy, the thick stew was delicious, as was the crusty bread. Johnny was hungry. And while he could enjoy the pleasure of the food, he had to steer clear of the woman who sat across the table.

STEPHANIE ATE THE STEW she'd cooked, but her thoughts weren't on the food. Johnny Kreel took center stage in her mind. For no reason at all, Familiar had attacked him under the table.

She tore off a crust of bread and chewed it slowly. She didn't know Familiar, but in a few short days, she'd come to trust him a lot more than she trusted Johnny Kreel.

The man's past employment checked out, but that didn't mean anything. That was the last six months. Where had he been the other thirty or so years of his life?

"Are you from this area, Johnny?"

"No, ma'am," he answered, gaze focused on his bowl.

"So where *are* you from?" She was like a dog worrying a bone when she got started. She'd know every detail before she was done.

"I grew up in the wire grass country of Alabama. My granddad raised cattle." He still didn't look at her.

"And what happened between growing up and today?"

At last he lifted his gaze, and she saw there was a tempest brewing in his oddly colored eyes. He covered it quickly.

"I went to the University of Alabama on a scholarship and ended up in the law school."

"You have a law degree?" She was surprised. Not that he didn't look capable. In fact, Johnny Kreel looked like he could take on and conquer almost anything he set his hand to.

"I do, but I only practiced for five years. It wasn't the job for me."

He'd really ignited her curiosity now. "Why not?"

Picking up a piece of bread, he took his time answering. She could see that he was thinking through his response, which meant he cared.

"I thought the law was going to be about fighting for truth and justice." The tiniest bit of red tinged his strong face. "I know that sounds corny, but it's true. I really thought I could make a difference."

He returned to his food as if he'd answered her.

"What happened?"

Johnny met her stare head-on. This time he didn't look away or flinch. "A man I defended—an innocent man— ended up in prison. He was killed before his case came up for appeal."

"I'm so sorry." An almost irresistible urge to put a comforting hand on his arm struck her, but she restrained herself.

"He was a good guy. An innocent man wrongly accused. Putting him in prison was like throwing him into the lion's den. Everyone knew he'd be killed and no one did a thing to stop it. After that, I sort of lost my taste for the justice system."

"A law degree can be a handy thing," she said. Rupert Casper and Black Jack sprang to mind. Wasn't there some law that said possession was nine-tenths of the law?

"I don't practice. Besides, I was only licensed in Alabama."

"You could get licensed here. Folks in town would be glad to have another lawyer."

"Not this one." The way he said it told her he was ready to let the subject drop.

"So after you quit the law, what did you do?"

He visibly relaxed. "I bummed around the country, working on ranches and doing odd jobs. I needed to get back in touch with the things I've always loved about the West."

"And did you?"

He finally laughed. "Did you work for the Spanish Inquisition in a past life?"

His question was so unexpected that she laughed, too. His dusty cowboy clothes hid a lot more than they revealed. "Maybe," she said. "You just never know, do you?"

"No, ma'am, you don't." He eased his empty bowl away

from him. "That was delicious, except for the wine I threw all over myself. Now if you'll excuse me, I'll make sure Tex is comfortable, stop by and visit with Black Jack for a moment and then I'll be off to bed."

Chapter Three

Stephanie swatted away the small furry creature that licked her face with a barbed-wire tongue. It took several moments to realize that a black cat was in her bed and demanding that she wake up. Pushing the cat away, she tried to sink back into a dream where a handsome cowboy walked through her barn and straight into her arms.

It took another moment to remember that Familiar was her houseguest.

She reached out to stroke Familiar's head. A soft chuckle escaped as she thought back through the events of the day before. The cat had really done a number on Rupert Casper. Familiar's "gift" to Black Jack's owner had been purr-fect. She kissed the top of Familiar's head and earned another sandpaper lick.

Too bad Black Jack was such a tough case. She sensed the horse's fear. He lashed out at humans because he'd been hurt, and hurt badly. Some horses could be "broken" by cruelty, punishment and pain. Others, like Black Jack, died fighting mistreatment. The question was, could she bring Black Jack back from the brink of self-destruction? She wanted to show him that humans could be kind and loving and a true partner. But would he accept that after the abuse he'd received?

As much as she hated the idea, she might have to confront Rupert Casper about what, exactly, he'd done to the horse. That knowledge would figure prominently in how she approached Black Jack.

With the memory of the stallion's bad behavior came thoughts of Johnny Kreel. She'd hired a cowboy. Johnny wasn't some phantom. He was flesh and blood, a handsome man who'd infiltrated her dreams.

She groaned and rolled over, cracking one eye open to find dawn breaking in the east.

"It's not even light outside," she complained to the cat. But Familiar had done a thorough job of waking her. She threw back the covers and put her feet on the chilly floor.

It was only October, but the mornings were cold. She found clean socks, jeans and her boots. From the dresser she pulled out a thick shirt and slipped it on. Feeding the stock was the first order of business.

Grabbing a jacket, she stepped out the back door into the crisp morning. In the distance the Black Hills rose from the flatland, a symbol of many things Stephanie loved. Her grandfather had been Oglala Sioux, and her ranch was named for him. Running Horse. He'd been legendary as a "gentler," a man who preferred the company of his horses to that of humans.

After the death of his wife, Running Horse had lived alone on a small ranch with his horses. His reputation had spread far and wide, and people drove from all over the continent to bring him horses.

They brought him the rank horses, the ones that no amount of training or abuse could break. Stephanie had never seen him agitated for a single moment. He studied each animal and learned the horse's secret wounds. Then he began the process of listening and building trust.

Stephanie had spent her summers following behind him like the most loyal of dogs. His days had been long, but Stephanie was never bored. She watched him work, listening to him talk about this horse's spirit or that horse's past experiences.

Not one single time had she ever complained of tiredness or hunger. Grandfather Running Horse and the privilege of sharing his work was all she needed.

Until she turned thirteen. Her life had unraveled then. The grandfather she adored was killed in a farming accident.

Stephanie's parents, both more interested in humanitarian efforts than money, couldn't afford to keep up the ranch, so it had been sold. Five years later, they died in a cholera epidemic in Africa. The tradition of horse gentling had almost died with Running Horse—until Stephanie decided to try her hand at it.

As Stephanie walked across the yard to the barn, she felt her grandfather's presence with her. She often felt him close by. In the long days since her fiancé had disappeared into the Central American jungles in a tragic plane crash, her grandfather's spirit had sustained her.

And he was with her now.

She heard the sound of hoofbeats and hurried into the barn. Tex and Layla peeked out of their stalls. Each gave a throaty greeting.

"In a minute," she said as she walked by. First she had to see who was running, and why. Concern drove her to pick up speed.

She burst out of the barn and stopped in her tracks. In

the round pen, Black Jack was moving at an extended trot. Muscles rippled beneath his glossy hide, and she was struck by the sheer beauty of the horse's movement. His grace and balance were exquisite.

In the center of the round pen was Johnny Kreel. He held a soft cotton rope in his hand, sometimes slapping it lightly against his leg when Black Jack slowed.

Stepping forward, he turned a shoulder to the horse and Black Jack stopped. His flowing mane settled on his neck and he snorted, a wary eye on Johnny's every move.

"Reverse," Johnny said crisply. He stepped forward, shifting his position again. The horse did an about-face and began to trot around the edge of the round pen in the opposite direction. Johnny moved back to the center and continued shifting so that he constantly faced the horse.

It all went as smooth as clockwork.

Stephanie walked to the round pen and put her boot on the rail. "Well done," she said softly. She didn't want to distract Johnny from his total focus on Black Jack.

"He understands what I tell him."

"I've never doubted his intelligence," Stephanie said. "I just wonder if he can overcome the way Rupert Casper handled him. From the stories I heard, it was pretty brutal."

"He can leave it behind," Johnny said. "That's our job—to see that he does."

She'd tried to block out Black Jack's future, but now she confronted it. "And once we straighten him out, he'll go back to Rupert Casper."

Johnny signaled the horse to whoa. Black Jack slowed to a walk and then stopped. He stood perfectly still as Johnny walked to Stephanie.

"Maybe not. Life is peculiar. Sometimes a horse ends up where he needs to be."

Stephanie wished that were true. "I can't afford to buy Black Jack, even if Rupert would consider selling him, which he won't. Black Jack is a high-dollar horse."

"He's not worth much if Rupert Casper can't ride him," Johnny pointed out as he vaulted over the rail and stood beside her.

"You heard Rupert. He'll see the horse dead before he lets anyone else ride him. That's the kind of man he is."

Johnny wiped the sweat from his forehead. "Let's see how far we get with Black Jack before we predict the future. Or maybe, as the folks in town say, you've got a crystal ball in the house. And a boiling kettle and a broom that flies."

Stephanie couldn't stop the frown. "Folks in town been talking about me, have they?"

"Folks don't mean harm," Johnny said. "Their lives are boring and they think yours isn't."

"I think they should mind their own business. But for your information, I don't practice witchcraft or black magic. Now I've got to feed the horses and you should see what you can do with Moon Stinger and Dolly's Rocker. They're both in the barn and both need some work."

"I'll take care of it," he said.

She left him at the round pen and continued with her morning barn chores. Feeding the horses was always a pleasure. She loved the snuffling noise they made as they cleaned up their oats.

When she started back to the house, she passed Johnny's rig parked beside the barn. The trailer was in excellent shape, and the truck was well maintained for a rodeo man.

She glanced at the interior as she walked by. Just

beneath the edge of the front seat was a gun. Not a rifle, which a lot of ranchers carried, but a handgun. Something that looked modern and dangerous.

She kept walking, unsure how the weapon made her feel. Guns were a part of life for many men. Somehow, though, she hadn't expected it with Johnny. He was different. He communicated with the horses. Folks like him normally didn't care to carry a deadly firearm.

Then again, she didn't know him. She couldn't forget that, no matter how much she admired his technique when he worked with the horses. He was an unknown entity, and chances were he wouldn't remain around Running Horse Ranch long enough for her to figure out who he was deep down.

THE DAY IS OFF to an excellent start. Cowboy Johnny is dealing with the devil horse, and Miss Cowgirl found the gun in the cab of Johnny's truck. Now, I'm not a gun aficionado, but I've seen a lot of weapons in my day. That is an expensive weapon. And one with some firepower. A Glock, one of the preferred weapons of law enforcement agencies and the Feds.

Which makes me wonder about a couple of things. How did Johnny find the Running Horse Ranch? We're miles off the beaten path. He had to drive here specifically. And he shows up with a skill set that just happens to be what Stephanie needs.

I've always been told not to look a gift horse in the mouth, but what if it's the Trojan horse? When something is too good to be true, it usually is. So now it's up to me to do a bit of sleuthing.

Is Johnny Kreel just a drifting cowboy, or is there more

to this package than meets the eye? Stephanie has a computer. I can start there. With my private investigator knowledge, I can check a few Web sites and start a background check on this guy.

But first some breakfast. I catch the aroma of bacon. While I'm normally a seafood kind of cat, I can be swayed by other dishes. A nice bacon and cheese omelet would do wonders for my hungry tummy.

Then off to work.

LIFTING THE OMELET from the skillet, Stephanie served the cat and then began making breakfast for Johnny. He'd finished with Black Jack and she'd called him in before he started work on the other two horses.

He sat at the table, though he'd offered to help cook. She kept looking at him, his dark hair slicked back and his face freshly shaved. With his strange gray-green eyes, he seemed to take in everything.

She put the omelet in front of him and sat down to finish her coffee and toast.

"Not hungry?" he asked.

"I don't normally eat breakfast," she said, "but Familiar let me know he was ready for something."

"Smart cat." Johnny glanced at the shelf where she kept her cookbooks and several framed photographs. "Is that your husband?" he asked, indicating a picture of Stephanie and a handsome man on a beach.

Stephanie didn't have to look at the photo to know what it was. It had been taken only weeks before she moved to South Dakota. She and Rory had been at Gulf Shores, Alabama, a last fling in the Southern sun before moving north. It was the last weekend Rory had been alive.

"My fiancé," she said. "He died in a plane crash." Normally that put the kibosh on further conversation.

"I'm sorry," Johnny said. "You two look so happy. When was the crash?"

She almost told him to mind his own business, but she stopped herself. "About four months ago. He ran a charter airline business out of New Orleans. His plane went down somewhere in the Darien Jungle."

Johnny stopped eating. "That must be terrible for you."

To her surprise, she found her eyes clouding with tears. "Rory was a good man. We were going to run this business together."

"He was giving up his charter business?"

She nodded. "He loved flying, but he could have kept one plane and done a part-time business here. Mostly, though, we wanted to focus on the horses."

"So he was a trainer, too."

Stephanie smiled. "Not really. But he wanted to learn. That's the important thing, isn't it? To want to learn a different way of relating to an animal."

"If more folks were willing to open their minds, it would be a different world," Johnny said. He wiped his mouth with a napkin. "I should get to work, but first…" He picked up his plate and went to the sink, where he ran the hot water and began washing up.

"That's not necessary," Stephanie said.

"Probably not. But you cooked, so I'll clean up. It's not a fifty-fifty distribution of work, but it's more fair than your doing it all."

She leaned back in her chair and sipped her coffee, watching him as he efficiently tidied the kitchen. He knew his way around housework, which was more than surprising for a cowboy.

"How long do you expect to be in these parts?" she asked.

Johnny didn't turn around. He rinsed a plate and set it in the drainer. "I'd thought a couple of weeks, but I'm in no hurry to leave. Nobody is expecting me anywhere down the line."

"That's good to know," she said. Winter was coming. While the ranch work was hard enough in the summer heat, the winter was going to be long and cold and even more difficult. "Maybe, if things work out, you'd want to stay around here."

"Let's get to the end of the first two weeks. After that, if you like the way I work, we can negotiate a salary."

"Perfect." She stood and took her coffee cup to the sink. "When you finish Dolly and Stinger, let me know. We'll saddle up and check the fence line on the north pasture."

He grinned. "Sounds like a good plan. I haven't done range work in a long time."

"You'll get plenty of chances around here," she said.

HE RODE CUTTING PATTERNS on Stinger and Dolly. Both horses moved willingly and with total confidence. Stephanie had done a wonderful job with them. If they'd had problems, he could find no trace of them.

When he was finished, he knocked at the back door, and Stephanie came out, ready to ride. The afternoon had warmed, and she carried a light jacket. They saddled two more horses and set out across the flatland toward the Black Hills.

He had questions to ask. Plenty of them. But he had to be careful how he phrased them. He could see that the wound Rory Sussex had left was still raw. And if Stephanie ever found out who and what Rory really was, she'd be terribly hurt. On one hand, Johnny could understand why Rory would lie. Stephanie was a rare woman. And she'd never have willingly involved herself with a man whose entire life was a web of fabrications. It was either lie or lose her.

But Rory had to know that eventually the house of cards would come tumbling down around him. He couldn't simply walk away from the life he'd led and become a different person. Certainly, he may have thought that the wilds of South Dakota were secluded enough that he could build a new life. But they weren't. And now Stephanie had been caught in Rory's past.

"You're looking mighty serious," she said as they crossed a dry creek bed. "Something wrong?"

"Sorry. I was thinking about your fiancé and his plane crash. It's just hard to grab hold of. Did they find out why the plane crashed?"

Stephanie waited until her horse had scrambled up the side of the creek bed before she answered. "They never found the plane. Or Rory's body. The control tower got a Mayday call from Rory. He was having engine trouble. That's the last anyone heard."

"They never found any of the wreckage?" Johnny knew this. The trouble was, he didn't believe it.

"No. I hired an investigator, someone who knew the jungle. They searched, but it's apparently impenetrable in places."

He could see that she was uncomfortable. It would be hard for anyone to count a loved one dead without a body. He hated the word *closure,* but it was true. The physical body gave closure, allowed death to become real.

Except, in the case of Rory Sussex, Johnny didn't believe there *had* been a plane crash or a death. In fact, he and the U.S. government were almost certain that Rory was very much alive.

The question was where had he gone and when would he show up at Running Horse Ranch?

Chapter Four

Sunlight glinted off something—a quick wink, wink. Johnny saw it, but he didn't call Stephanie's attention to it. Someone was on the high north ridge, watching them with binoculars.

He eased his horse forward so he was between Stephanie and the watcher. Just in case.

So who was it on the ridge? Was it Rory? Or was it some of the men pursuing Rory? Johnny had no doubt that members of Carlos Diego's gang were hot on Rory's heels. Rory had managed to piss off everyone involved. And Diego, a powerful man who'd built an empire selling information and drugs, didn't keep hurt feelings to himself. He resolved his problems with bullets.

"Here's a break in the fence." Stephanie slipped off her horse, put on her gloves and began pulling the barbed wire out of a tangle. She used her lithe body to tug the wire taut, and Johnny was momentarily captivated by her sheer physical beauty.

When she looked up at him with a frown, he dismounted and grasped the wire to help her. She labored with total concentration, and Johnny could see that she'd learned to work fast and efficiently. Living alone on a South Dakota ranch, she had no time for mistakes or leisure.

"Something wrong?" she asked.

He found her staring at him, brown eyes puzzled. A whisper of suspicion shifted across her features.

"No. Just distracted for a moment." He forced his mind back to the job at hand.

"Distracted by what?" she asked.

"Thinking about how you'll manage here by yourself." He saw instantly that he'd offended her. Her cheeks flushed with anger and she yanked at the wire.

"I'll manage just fine. A man isn't the solution to every problem on a ranch, you know."

He controlled the impulse to touch her and wondered what was wrong with him. He'd almost stroked her back, as if it were his job to comfort her, as if she'd desired his protection. "I didn't mean it that way. If you were a man, I'd still have concerns about one person with all this work and responsibility. What if you get hurt? Cell phone coverage out here is spotty at best. You could lie—"

"Stop it!" She wheeled around to confront him. "Stop it right now. A meteorite could fall out of the sky and strike me if I lived in Chicago or New York. A driver could have a heart attack and lose control of a car and I could be crushed. Or someone could mug me. The only difference is that I'd likely lie in the middle of the street with people passing by and no one would help."

"I'm sorry, Stephanie. I didn't mean to upset you." He could see that he'd stepped in it deep. An apology wasn't going to smooth this over.

"Bad things happen everywhere, Johnny. It's true, I could get hurt here. But I could get hurt anywhere. And just let me tell you, for the record, the worst kind of hurt comes not from physical pain but from—" She broke off and took a deep breath.

"I didn't mean to sound macho or condescending."

She struggled to regain control of her emotions, and he could see how much it cost her. "It's okay. I overreacted."

She bent back to the fence, and he had an opportunity to scan the ridge. There was no reflection of sunlight on metal. Whoever had been watching had either left or hidden.

While he didn't like it, he had expected it. Rory Sussex had stolen from two factions—the U.S. government and Carlos Diego. Both were out to get him.

And Stephanie was caught squarely in the middle— with the added handicap that she had no clue as to what was happening around her.

"Let's keep moving," she said as he helped her pull the fence tight and stapled it into place. "I want to cover this north line before dark."

"Yes, ma'am," he answered, glad for any reason to move away from the ridge where the observer had such an advantage.

He wasn't worried that someone would hurt Stephanie. Not yet. Not until Rory made his next move. But once Rory initiated the action, Stephanie could become the bone in a very big dogfight.

STEPHANIE REGRETTED HER OUTBURST, but she was fed up with folks heaping doom and gloom on her head. She knew the risks and dangers of living alone, so isolated, on a horse ranch. Once the winter set in, travel was difficult and there was no guarantee anyone would think to check on her. But the truth was, she could just as easily live in town and be alone. She hadn't bothered to try to make friends, and there was no one to miss her even if she lived in a town apartment and were injured.

She blew her breath out, mounted her horse and rode along the fence. They mended an additional two breaks and finally hit the end of the fence line. The wire was good for another winter, unless a deer or something crashed through it and took it down.

They'd worked in silence for the better part of an hour, and she'd grown comfortable with him. As she turned her horse toward the barn, Johnny spoke again.

"I am sorry if I upset you."

"It wasn't you. Every time I go into town, I hear that. People feel compelled to warn me about all the dire things that might happen. I don't see them fretting about Wade Chisholm or Will Tanner. And it's because they're men. Because I'm a woman who's chosen this life, they can't help but see me as reckless."

To her surprise, he chuckled. "Point taken. You trust yourself, and others should respect that and trust your decisions."

Despite the fact that she was still a little sore, she laughed, too, though her laugh was rueful. "Sometimes trust can be misplaced."

"Folks can disappoint—that's a fact. I'd rather spend my time with a horse," Johnny agreed.

"A horse and one black cat." She relaxed, letting her body sway with Flicker's movement as the little roan carried her home. "You know, I never thought I'd be a cat person, but Familiar is so…"

"Intelligent?" Johnny supplied.

"That's right. He seems to hear everything I say and he

even answers me. I'm sure he does." She laughed out loud. "Eleanor, his owner, says he's a detective. That people around the world hire him to solve cases."

A frown passed over Johnny's face. "Really? How extraordinary."

"You don't think it's poppycock?"

"Why couldn't it be true?" Johnny shrugged. "It's as likely as some of the things I've seen."

She found it surprisingly easy to talk to Johnny. Before he'd appeared at Running Horse Ranch, weeks had passed when she didn't speak to anyone. Once she stocked up on supplies, she only went to town for emergencies or necessities. And she'd spent most of July and August on the ranch.

"Tell me about Black Jack," Johnny said. "Where did Rupert Casper get him and how?"

Stephanie thought back through the tangle of the horse's history. "Some of this is fact and some is gossip and some is pure vicious rumor from the two men who brought Black Jack here."

"Let's start with the vicious rumor. That's my favorite part," Johnny said.

Stephanie took a swat at his arm. "Could be you're working for the local gossip mill in town and have been sent here to get the real story on me."

"Is there a real story?" Johnny asked.

The question caught her by surprise, especially since he watched her with the keenest look. Almost as if he expected her to reveal some deep, dark secret. Well, he'd be mighty disappointed if that was what he was waiting for. She'd had tragedy, for sure, but nothing she had any desire to reveal.

"What you see is what you get," she said. "Now let's talk about the horse."

"I'm listening."

"Gibb and Kyle brought Black Jack over about two weeks ago. They said there'd been an accident. Rupert decided he was going to ride Black Jack whether the horse wanted it or not. They saddled him, and Rupert got on." She watched Johnny's expression, trying to gauge his feelings, but she couldn't read him. It was as if a mask had settled over his features.

"Black Jack was quick and vicious and he threw Rupert and then stomped Rupert's shoulder," she continued. "Rupert felt that the horse meant to kill him, so he ordered the horse to be shot. While Rupert was in the hospital, Gibb and Kyle brought him here to me. They said Rupert had struck him repeatedly with a club. They believed the horse was merely trying to defend himself."

Johnny sighed. "I guess he thought he'd beat the horse into submission."

"Something I'd like to try on Rupert," Stephanie said darkly.

"So where did Black Jack come from originally?"

"From Nevada. An actor named Jim Diamond had a big cutting horse ranch. He died and his son sold everything. He didn't care about the ranch or the stock or any of it. He wanted the cash. Black Jack had a reputation for being difficult to handle even then. But Jim Diamond loved him, and the horse was obedient and well-behaved for him."

"Horses know when people care about them."

Stephanie nodded. "That's true. Anyway, Black Jack had a couple of homes before Rupert got him. There were incidents, and people were injured trying to handle the stallion. He acquired a reputation—and not a good one. So Rupert got him for way under value." In the distance the ranch was visible. She'd be glad to get home.

"And Rupert would rather kill him than let him go to someone who could help him?"

"Rupert has an ego the size of California and a brain smaller than a pea."

"I didn't care for what I saw of him."

"I'd love to bury him in an ant bed and coat his head with honey."

Johnny's laughter was rich and deep. "I hope I don't ever piss you off," he said.

She glared at him but couldn't hold it. "See that you don't." But then she spoiled the effect by laughing herself.

"Anyway, Black Jack is a descendent of Three Bars and Iron Man. He's working cattle all the way, and if someone can get through to him, he'll be one of the fanciest, finest cow horses in the West."

"We made some progress this morning."

She flashed him a smile. "I saw that. But don't let him trick you. He's smart and he doesn't trust people. He'll act fine for several days, and then he'll snap."

That put a frown on the cowboy's face.

"You don't think he's unbalanced, do you?" Johnny asked.

Stephanie gave that thought serious consideration. She owed Johnny that much if he was going to put himself at risk by working the stallion. "I don't think so. I believe he's terribly smart. And he watches us. But his trust has been undermined. If we can't teach him to trust again, I don't know that he'll ever be reliable."

"We'll see what tomorrow brings," Johnny said. "Race you to the barn."

He didn't give her a chance to accept or decline. His gelding spurted forward and Stephanie had no choice but to lean forward into Flicker's mane or eat his dust.

WHILE THE HUMANS are away, the cat will play. At least this black cat will. Thank goodness it's a beautiful, sunny day. I need to do some work on the Internet, and reception might be problematic if the atmosphere is cloudy. Way out here in the hinterlands, the only Internet access is by satellite.

It's a simple matter to check out Johnny Kreel, cowboy extraordinaire. I like it that he's here to help Miss Cowgirl, but the more I've thought about the coincidence of his arrival, the more troubled I've become.

Let's see here. Johnny Kreel, born Oct. 30, 1973. Almost a Halloween baby. Born to Patricia and John Kreel in Enterprise, Alabama.

Attended the University of Alabama and graduated from law school. Interesting.

Not a whole lot of additional information. No service record. Nothing suspicious, and nothing of any real interest. Homogenized work record, and then he sort of vanishes from the Internet. Let me check the rodeo rosters.

Here he is, just where he said he'd been. Followed the rides along Texas, Oklahoma, and into South Dakota. Okay, he checks out so far.

But someone who wanted to create a past could do so without too much trouble. And why am I suspicious? Call it a hunch. Or call it an observation, if that pleases you more. While I'm glad he showed up and rescued Miss Cowgirl, I can't help but find it odd that he appears out of the clear blue sky—a man who finds his way to a horse ranch at the end of miles of dead-end dirt roads.

Could be simple coincidence or good luck. Could be a higher power at work. Or it could be that Johnny Kreel set out to find Stephanie for some as-yet-unrevealed purpose. I don't have the answer to that, but my gut has kept me alive more times than I can count.

Speaking of gut, I think it's dinnertime. And lo and behold, here come the range-riding cowhands. Thank goodness they didn't invite me to go and mend fences. I was far happier poking around the house. Now let me shut this computer down before they realize I've been checking up on things.

AT STEPHANIE'S DIRECTION, Johnny washed his hands at the kitchen sink and took the hand towel she proffered. To his embarrassment, his stomach registered a loud complaint.

"Sounds like you're hungry," Stephanie said. "Me, too. Let's see what kind of grub we can throw together."

"I can cook." Johnny spoke before he thought. She slowly faced him, an amused grin reflected in her dancing eyes.

"Oh, really? A cowboy who has a law degree and who cleans up the kitchen and can cook." She folded the dish towel carefully. "That's not a combination of talents one normally finds in South Dakota."

Johnny felt the blood climbing his cheeks. Before he could say anything, she shook her head.

"And one who blushes. My, my."

"Damn it." He ran his hand through his hair. "You are one aggravating woman." To his chagrin, that amused her even more.

"I've been called a lot worse," she said. "That aside, how about some steaks and the fixings?"

"Perfect," he said.

They worked together and whipped up the meal in short

order. When Johnny questioned the third steak, Stephanie pointed at the cat.

"Familiar likes steak."

She was setting the table when the telephone rang. She picked it up as she searched through a drawer for steak knives. "Running Horse Ranch," she said.

Johnny pulled two chilled beers from the refrigerator and was putting them on the table when he heard the phone clatter to the floor.

Stephanie was white as a ghost.

"What's wrong?" he asked.

She looked as if she were going into shock. He grasped her elbow and supported her while at the same time scooping up the telephone.

"Who is this?" he demanded into the phone.

"Stay out of this," a muffled and distorted male voice said. "This is between me and the woman."

Johnny felt the adrenaline run through him. This was the first move. The finish could prove very bloody. "Who is this?" he repeated.

"The man who's going to gut you like a dead animal if you don't clear off that ranch and mind your own business."

Instead of answering, Johnny ended the call. Stephanie had recovered, and he saw spots of anger in her cheeks.

"That bastard," she said.

"Who was it?"

"It doesn't matter." She started to turn away, but Johnny grasped her shoulders.

"Who was it?" Johnny insisted.

"Let me go." Stephanie's eyes flashed danger.

Johnny held her firmly. "What did he say?"

She struggled for a moment before she stopped. When

she met his gaze, her eyes were hard as flint. "He said he was watching me."

Johnny kept his features bland, just as he'd been trained. "Did he say anything else?"

She shook her head. "That was enough. And that tactic won't work on me. It'll be a cold day in hell before Rupert Casper gets the better of me with a threatening phone call."

For a moment Johnny was stunned. "Rupert Casper?"

"That's who was on the phone. Who else would call here and say he's watching me, like he's some kind of killer waiting for an opportunity to strike?" Stephanie clattered two plates onto the table. "Well, he can't frighten me with that foolishness."

Johnny opened the two beers, taking his time. "You really think that was Casper?"

She got flatware from a drawer and finished the table settings. "Who else? It just shows what kind of bully he is."

"Why would he do that?" Johnny asked.

"Because he's gone back to his ranch and sulked about Black Jack. He realized that he made himself look like a fool. Now he's going to make me pay because I didn't let him kill the horse." She motioned Johnny into a chair as she put the food on the table. "Did he say anything to you?"

Johnny hesitated. Now was the time to come clean, to tell Stephanie everything. He didn't for a minute believe the man on the other end of the telephone was Rupert Casper. Not a chance. The caller was someone far more lethal, and by not telling Stephanie, he put her at risk. But ignorance of the events unfolding around her might also be her only way to stay safe. "No, not a word."

She'd cut up one of the steaks into bite-size portions for

Familiar, and she set it on the table. The black cat hopped onto a chair and sat, golden eyes watching Johnny carefully.

"Then let's eat. That goat isn't going to spoil my supper." Stephanie slipped into a chair and unfolded her napkin. "Dig in."

Johnny picked up his fork, but he found himself staring into the golden gaze of the cat. Familiar was glaring at him, as if the cat knew he'd lied.

He speared a bite of steak and forced himself to eat. He'd come to Running Horse Ranch with an assignment, and despite his personal feelings, he was duty bound to follow this through to the end. Exactly as he'd been ordered. He had no other choice.

Chapter Five

Stephanie felt someone stabbing needles into her cheeks. She fought against them, her hand clutching something soft and furry. With a scream, she sat up in bed and snapped on the bedside lamp.

"Yeow!" Familiar swatted her face, and not with gentleness.

"Stop it." She tried to brush the cat off the bed, but he was frantic.

"Yeow!" he insisted.

Something in the feline's eyes frightened her. She threw back the covers and stood on the cold floor.

"Yeow!" Familiar was dragging her jeans to her. Next he was pulling a boot over.

She took the hint and dressed quickly. "What is it?" she asked the cat.

He led the way out of the bedroom and to the kitchen.

The minute she entered the room, she knew what was wrong. The kitchen window framed a scene from hell. Across the yard, flames shot into the black night.

"The barn!" Liquid fear jetted through her veins, and for a moment she was frozen in panic. When she felt the cat's sharp claws in her calf, she bolted into action.

No point calling for help. The fire department was too far away. The only thing to do was get the horses out. And fast.

Forgoing a jacket, she rushed into the night, stopping only to batter the door of the bunkhouse. "Fire! Fire!" she cried, then dashed toward the barn.

The nights had not yet grown cold, so luckily the barn doors were open. She rushed inside, opening the stalls for Tex and Layla as she passed.

Panicked, the horses spun in their stalls, too afraid to go through the open door.

Stephanie thought of her grandfather, of the first rule he'd ever taught her. A horse picks up on a human's fear, and that makes for a dangerous, unstable horse. She had to get a grip on herself.

"Layla." She extended her hand and softly captured the mare's halter. "It's okay, Layla." Though she could hear the roar of the fire growing louder, she concentrated on that one moment, that one horse. This was her golden palomino, her friend. They'd ridden the range together many times. She forced that image into her head and held on to it.

Layla calmed enough for Stephanie to lead her through the open stall door and into the night. When Stephanie turned her loose, Tex followed her to freedom.

The horses at the west end of the barn were in the most danger. Flicker, Nugget, Mirage, Cimarron and Dasher were screaming in fear. She could see the fire running along the back wall of Cimarron's stall.

Smoke began to fill the barn, and she pulled her shirt up to cover her mouth and nose. She was about to plunge deeper into the barn when a human cannonball passed her. Johnny Kreel was moving at a dead run, and he ran straight into the flames.

"Johnny!" She took off after him. While he worked the stall doors on the right, she opened the ones on the left. There was no time now for visualization or calm. If the horses didn't get out—if she and Johnny didn't get out—they'd be burned to death.

Cimarron, Nugget and Flicker ran, but she could see that Dasher was spinning in his stall, crazy with fear and panic. Johnny kept reaching for him, but the horse was beyond reasoning.

"Let me," she said, walking straight into the stall, totally confident in the little chestnut she'd raised from a colt. "Easy, boy," she said. Her fingers caught his halter, and with one smooth motion, she was on his back. "Mirage will follow him," she said. "Come on!" She gave Johnny her hand and he swung up behind her.

It took no pressure to encourage Dasher forward. He trusted her, and when she asked, he lunged through the open stall door and was out of the barn in two strides, Mirage right on his heels.

Choking and coughing, they continued into the cold night until they were well away from the barn. They stopped where the other horses, still afraid and confused, milled and whinnied.

"I'll get Black Jack out of the other barn," Johnny said as he slid to the ground. "I don't think there's any danger that the fire will spread to his barn, but he's bound to be terrified by the flames."

"Be careful. I'll put these guys in the corral," Stephanie said. Behind her, the barn was a total loss. The flames had crept across the roof and were steadily reducing to ash the structure into which she'd poured most of her life savings.

Away from the fire and the panic, she realized that she

was shivering. The night was crisp and cold and perfectly clear. Not a cloud in the sky. Which meant the barn fire was not started by lightning.

As she put the horses into the big corral, she fought against the tears of frustration that threatened to overwhelm her. Crying would do no good. She'd learned that a long time ago. Crying didn't do anything except stop up her nose and make her feel worse.

The horses were safe. That was the thing that mattered. Barns could be rebuilt. Saddles could be replaced. Those were only things. The living creatures she'd come to love were safe.

She heard hooves on the hard ground and watched as Johnny and Black Jack, silhouettes against the flames, walked calmly to the big round pen. Black Jack entered with the docility of a lamb. Johnny fastened the gate and headed her way.

Swallowing back her emotions, she squared her shoulders. When Johnny approached and put an arm around her, she didn't object.

"You need a coat," he said, taking his off and putting it on her.

"And you don't?" she asked.

To her surprise, his hand touched her jaw with great tenderness. "I'll get one from the bunkhouse in a minute." He shifted so that he watched the barn burn. "I tried to put in a 9-1-1 call to the fire department."

"Phone reception is out, right?"

He inhaled. "Yeah. There's nothing they could do anyway, except file a report for your insurance. Let's make some coffee and let the fire burn out. There's no wind and the other buildings are safe."

She had no argument left in her. Trudging beside him, she went into the kitchen. She'd put on the coffeepot before she realized the black cat was nowhere in sight.

"Where's Familiar?" she asked, looking around the house and calling his name.

"There he is." Johnny pointed out the window. Familiar stalked the perimeter of the fire. "It actually looks like he's hunting for something."

"For evidence," Stephanie said.

"You're saying this fire was arson?"

Stephanie faced him. "This wasn't an accident. There was no lightning, and I can tell you that wasn't an electrical fire. The barn was brand new and the wiring was above code. Someone burned my barn to the ground, and if Familiar is a real detective, as Eleanor says, he's going to help me find the bastard who did this. And then that person is going to pay."

JOHNNY PULLED THE BLANKET over Stephanie's sleeping form. She'd gone through anger, grief and finally acceptance over the barn. Now she was finally sleeping on the sofa. And he had work to do.

Familiar was curled at Stephanie's side, but the moment Johnny started toward the door, the cat was following in his tracks. Johnny wasn't certain he believed that Familiar was actually a detective, but the cat had an uncanny ability to sense things. That much he was willing to concede.

Johnny refilled the watering troughs for the horses and checked over them in the pink light of a new day. While they snorted and danced, still anxious after the fire, none had suffered any injuries. Black Jack was fine, too, munching on the bale of hay that Johnny had thrown him.

Johnny walked around the steel skeleton of the barn. The support structure was probably okay, but the stalls were gone and winter wasn't far away. He knew enough about insurance companies to know that Stephanie would never get the funds to rebuild before the first snows hit.

She might be able to double up some horses in stalls in the other barn, but it was going to greatly complicate her winter.

He kept his thoughts focused in that direction as he walked around the smoldering building. The cat darted ahead of him and sat down.

"Meow." Familiar looked over his shoulder, as if he wanted to make sure Johnny was headed his way.

"What've you got?" Johnny knelt down and examined the ground where the cat waited.

Familiar lightly batted a piece of half-burned lumber. Out of curiosity, Johnny carefully lifted the wood. A bootprint was clearly visible. "Well, I'll be damned," he said, half to himself. He studied the tread. This wasn't a cowboy boot or a riding boot. This print had treads. More like a hiking boot.

He put his own foot beside it. And the owner of the print was a big man with big feet.

"Meow!"

Familiar moved. He patted the ground with his paw.

Johnny followed the cat and found another print. This one for the opposite foot. And the space between the two was a good four feet. The owner of the boots had quite a stride, which indicated a long-legged man.

Carlos Diego had a henchman who went by the name of Plenty. He was six foot eight and had a reputation for enjoying dishing out physical pain. Johnny stood up and surveyed the horizon. The idea that Plenty—or any of Diego's men—were out there, watching, made him antsy.

"Meow." Familiar rubbed against his legs.

"Good work, fella." He patted the cat's sleek coat. As difficult as it was to believe, Johnny couldn't deny that the cat had found the evidence.

Now Johnny could prove that someone had been on the property, but that was as far as it went. To get law enforcement action, he'd have to prove that the barn fire was arson. He had no doubt about that, and he was certain who was behind it—the same man who'd called earlier in the evening to intimidate Stephanie. The call she'd attributed to Rupert Casper, but Johnny knew better.

The sound of a truck starting made him glance behind him. Stephanie was not only awake, she was dressed and driving like she was fit to be tied.

"Hey!" He ran toward the truck.

"I'll be back," Stephanie yelled through the open window.

"Wait a minute." He flagged her down and stepped in front of the truck so she had to slow. "Where are you going?" He spoke as he walked toward the truck. When he saw the gun on the front seat, he knew where Stephanie was heading.

"Hold on there, Ms. Ryan," he said calmly.

"That man burned my barn to the ground. My horses could have died."

"But they didn't." Johnny felt as if he were on top of a powder keg. Stephanie was about to explode, and by withholding the truth from her, he would be guilty of lighting the fuse.

"Because Familiar woke me up. That cat saved my horses. And you. You saved them, too. But that crazy fool set fire to my barn, and I'm going to go over there and make him so sorry he'll wish I'd shoot him and put an end to his misery."

Johnny put a hand on the truck door. "Please don't do this."

"And why not?"

Here, again, was the perfect chance to tell her the truth. But he couldn't. He'd given his word. He'd taken an oath. And if she knew, she might be in even bigger danger. Stephanie wasn't the kind of person who took things lying down. She'd react. And because he couldn't control her reaction, he couldn't afford to tell her the truth.

"Because we need to prove who is behind this."

"I know damn well who's behind this and so do you. Rupert Casper."

Johnny almost corrected her, but he didn't. In all his years as an agent, he'd never betrayed his oath. "We need physical evidence, and we need to take it to the sheriff. Once we establish the person responsible for this, we can take action to put him in jail."

He could see that his logical approach sounded a lot to her like doing nothing. "Stephanie, this is the safest way for Black Jack. If you go over there and stir that hornet's nest, you'd better be prepared to get stung. He'll be over here with a bullet for that horse so quick your head will spin."

That, at last, penetrated her fury. She slowly reached for the key and turned off the engine. "I'm not going to let him get away with this."

"And I'm not saying that you should. But let's find the evidence. Let's do this the right way."

She swallowed, and for one instant there were bright tears in her eyes. She blinked them away. "If we don't get the evidence quickly, I'll handle this my way."

"And I'll help," he said, regretting those words the instant they left his mouth.

STANDING AT THE KITCHEN WINDOW, washing the coffee cups that had accumulated as the law officers and the insurance adjuster came and went, Stephanie tried not to think about the coming winter.

Her insurance adjuster had made it clear that until the issue of arson was settled, no claim would be paid. That meant no money to rebuild, possibly for months. She'd have to find a way to protect her herd from the bitter cold.

Sheriff Dobbs Petersen had noted two footprints and taken molds. The arson investigator he'd brought in had found traces of accelerant. There was no doubt that someone had deliberately set her barn on fire. Never in a million years had Stephanie anticipated that she and Johnny Kreel would become the prime suspects. That they'd rescued the horses counted for nothing. She and Johnny had means, opportunity and, because of the insurance policy, motive. It chapped her backside to think that anyone would believe she'd risk her horses or endanger herself and others for money.

She saw Johnny and Familiar cross the yard. The cat followed behind Johnny as if he were herding the ranch hand. And Familiar had found the footprints. She felt the corners of her mouth tug into a smile. Johnny was coming to recognize that the cat was something very special indeed.

She had no doubts now. Familiar had awakened her. Had he not… She couldn't bear to think what would have happened to her horses.

Another bout of emotion crested over her, and she gripped the sink, fighting the memories of Rory and the horror of his death. She'd quit her job in Liz Terrell Advertising Agency in preparation for the move to South Dakota, and she'd been packing up her New Orleans apartment when the two men from the Federal Aviation Administration knocked at her door.

The memory was bitingly clear. She'd slipped out of her dirty T-shirt and put on something more presentable before she answered the door. She'd been mildly curious, because she didn't expect anyone. Rory was on his last mission— a flight from the Panama Canal Zone to Colombia. He'd made the flight a thousand times before. He'd sold all but two of his airplanes. The engagement, the move to South Dakota, the building of their dream—everything was running smoothly.

She opened the doors, surprised at the solemn formality of the two men. And they'd told her. "I'm sorry to inform you, Ms. Ryan, but Rory Sussex's plane is missing and is believed to have crashed in the Darien Jungle."

That one sentence had changed her life drastically.

She'd questioned them, tried to gather details, but there were none. The plane was never found. Rory's body was never found. The jungle, impenetrable in places, had refused to yield the evidence that would settle the matter of Rory's death. Not even the private investigator she'd hired had been able to find anything. Rory's death was open and shut—for the U.S. government, at least. No one had shown the slightest interest in proving that he was dead.

She'd been left to live with the uncertainty. When someone talked about the need for closure, she now understood how important that was. Yet she'd come to accept that for her there would be no closure. She'd invested everything she had in Running Horse Ranch, and she'd had no choice but to move to South Dakota and make a go of it.

And now the barn was gone. She and Rory had drawn the plans for the building, and she'd hired the crew to make it a reality. Now there was nothing left of it. Johnny told her the steel structure seemed sound, but a building inspector would have to agree. That was weeks away. The debris had to be cleared first.

Closing her eyes against a wall of weariness, she took deep breaths. Her grandfather had faced circumstances as hard or harder. He hadn't quit. Neither would she. She'd get through this, and thank goodness for Johnny Kreel.

Providence had sent him to her, and she was more grateful than she'd ever let him know.

Chapter Six

Methinks there's something afoot here at Running Horse Ranch, and it doesn't bode well for Miss Cowgirl. I've watched a lot of law enforcement types work a crime scene, and while Johnny Kreel pretends he doesn't know much, that's just not so. He's very careful not to show his expertise, but he's savvy. He let me find the footprints, but I don't believe for a minute he wasn't already looking for them.

He's sandbagging the situation, and whenever a biped doesn't take credit for what he knows, to quote literary icon Will, something is rotten in Denmark.

Which begs the question, why? Why is he hiding his abilities and why does he have those abilities in the first place? Most cowboys—or lawyers for that matter—wouldn't know their way around a crime scene. No need. Not part of their job descriptions. Law enforcement officers and crime scene personnel work the scene, which is exactly what Johnny was doing, even if he hid it.

When Sheriff Petersen first showed up, Johnny didn't say a word. But he watched everything and then he asked questions, which led the investigators straight to the conclusion that the fire was arson. He also asked the insur-

ance adjustor some pointed questions, moving him down the same path. Johnny knows a lot about how law enforcement and insurance functions, which goes against his "Aw, shucks, I'm just a drifting cowpoke" image.

Now Johnny is saddling up, saying he's going out to check a fence line. But my guess is that he has other business, too. Which is fine by me, because as soon as he's gone, I'm hitting the bunkhouse for a bit of black cat sleuthing. If there's anything to be found in his gear, I'll unearth it.

Miss Cowgirl believes the fire was set by Rupert Casper, and Johnny has let her believe that. But my sixth sense tells me something different. There's another layer to this. Another dangerous level. Miss Cowgirl may be caught in something she has no clue about. But innocence has never been a valid defense—or protection.

It's my duty to look out for her, and that's one thing I take even more seriously than food.

There goes Johnny. I'll saunter over to the bunkhouse and see what I can find out.

WHEN JOHNNY RODE UP the first rise, he turned back to face Running Horse Ranch. The black ruins of the barn stood stark against the brown landscape. Anger made him tighten his grip on the saddle horn, and Cimarron shifted beneath him, sensing his sudden mood change.

He relaxed. No point unsettling the horse. His anger would serve no useful purpose. He had to concede that he was angrier at himself than at anyone else. Stephanie Ryan was in a dangerous place, and he was as guilty as anyone else because he'd failed to warn her.

But how could he tell her that everything she'd ever

believed about Rory Sussex was a lie? What would the truth do to her?

He silently cursed Rory for being so selfish as to involve Stephanie in his life. He'd chosen a certain path, one that didn't allow for the normal joys of family and community. His reward should have been knowing that he served his country. Instead, Rory had abandoned his oath and chosen greed and monetary gain, and in doing so, he'd betrayed his friends and coworkers and the United States of America.

Johnny had given it a lot of thought, and he'd seen how easy it must have been for Rory to pull off a double life. Stephanie was so focused on building a dream, carrying on her grandfather's work and teaching people how to have a better relationship with their horses that she didn't see trickery.

She was honest through and through, and that made it easy to deceive her. She'd never imagined that Rory wasn't exactly who he said he was. She'd never even thought to look into his background or check out the stories he told her.

Some would call it naive, but Johnny saw it another way. Stephanie lived in a world far different from the one he inhabited. His world was dark and ugly, and filled with violence and men who committed cruel acts out of greed.

Her world focused on the natural life, on her unique talents and abilities, and on her desire to help others, whether four-legged or two. She wasn't naive, she was good. There was a big difference.

Yet she would still pay the price. A price even higher than physical harm. She'd learn that she'd been betrayed by someone she loved.

Cimarron shifted restlessly, and he knew the horse was yet again picking up on his intense emotion. Horses could read a person's thoughts and intentions, just as Cimarron understood intuitively that he was angry and in need of physical release. It was time to get busy.

Pointing the mare to the north, Johnny set out at an easy lope for the fence he and Stephanie had been repairing. He wasn't worried about the wire, but he hoped to find some evidence of the watcher on the ridge.

If there were any way to handle this messy situation Rory Sussex had created and spare Stephanie from the truth, he intended to find it.

STEPHANIE SAW THE LONE HORSEMAN on the ridge and recognized Johnny. Even at that distance, she admired the way he sat in the saddle. He had real grace, and a talent for communicating with animals that matched her own skills.

No matter that the barn was gone; there was still work to be done. The hay supply was safe in the back barn, but most of her feed had been destroyed. She had enough for a couple of days, but the fire necessitated a trip to Custer. Dammit. She'd be happy not to go to town again until spring. And where in the world would she store her feed now? Too many questions and no simple answers.

She left the house and walked to the stud barn where Black Jack waited for her, his head out of the stall as if he were glad to see her.

She approached him with a lead rope and he willingly let her snap it on to his halter. He came out of the stall with a docile attitude.

She put him in the cross ties, picked up a brush and set to work on his gleaming coat. He was a true black, a horse so inky she could see her reflection in the gloss of his coat. A white cycle and star marked his handsome forehead.

Soon his winter hair would grow in, but now he looked like a show horse.

When she walked around him, he nuzzled her shoulder and she reached up to scratch below his ear. It was too soon to be certain, but it appeared that Black Jack had turned a corner.

And he was never going back to Rupert Casper. Hell would freeze over first.

"I'll keep you safe," she whispered against the horse's neck. She didn't know how, but she would.

Even as she thought Casper's name, Black Jack's attitude changed. He laid his ears back and bared his teeth, stomping a front hoof.

"Easy, boy. That's one worry you can let go of." She finished grooming him and led him to a paddock where he could run for several hours. Mostly in the warm-weather months, when the grass was sweet, she preferred to let the horses out on the range, where they could graze as they were meant to. But Black Jack wasn't trustworthy, and as a stallion, special precautions had to be taken to ensure his safety and to protect the other members of her herd.

She was walking back to the barn when she saw Casper's black truck headed her way. Her first instinct was to get her gun and shoot him as soon as he set foot on her property, but she remembered Johnny's words. The cowhand was right. She had to let the law handle this. If she committed an act of violence, she'd end up in jail and there would be no one to care for the animals that relied on her.

Familiar materialized at her side. She was amazed at the comfort the feline gave her. "You'd better skedaddle," she told the cat. "Rupert isn't likely to forget that you peed in his truck."

Familiar looked up at her and blinked. He rubbed against her legs and sauntered toward the bunkhouse.

Had he understood her? Stephanie wondered. It certainly seemed like it.

The black truck pulled up in a cloud of dust. Rupert Casper, his mother-of-pearl snap shirt buttons glinting in the sun, got out and walked to her side.

"Bad news about the barn," he said, nodding at the blackened structure. "Thought I'd take Black Jack home, get one horse off your hands."

Stephanie jerked a thumb in the direction of the paddock. "He's fine and making good progress. See for yourself." The stallion turned his tail toward Casper. It was a perfect comment on the man.

Casper flushed, and Stephanie was happy to see that he read the horse's insult. "The sheriff says the barn fire was arson." She put it out there, hoping for some reaction.

Casper was cool. "That's too bad. Who've you pissed off, Ms. Ryan?" He chuckled. "I mean half the county thinks you're a witch and the other half thinks you're a crazy recluse. But neither of those impressions sounds like a reason to burn down your barn."

"Is there ever a legitimate reason to burn down a building with animals in it?" she asked, aware that her words had some heat in them.

"Did you get all the horses out?"

She nodded, forcing herself to remain calm. "Everyone is fine. The insurance will rebuild the barn, and the sheriff will catch whoever started it. The culprit will be prosecuted to the fullest extent of the law."

"Well, that's the way to handle it." Rupert walked over to the ruins. "So it was arson."

"That's right."

He kicked an ember. "I wonder how they tell that. Looks like a pile of rubble to me."

"An accelerant was used. Whoever set the fire wasn't very bright. The sheriff will trace the accelerant and find who purchased that particular type. The guilty party will be rooted out." She watched Casper carefully. If she couldn't slug him, at least she'd arouse some anxiety in him, for she had no doubt that he was behind the fire.

"I'm heading into Missoula today," he said, "but I can send Gibb to get Black Jack if he's a bother."

"He's doing just fine. I'm going to ride him this afternoon." She hadn't really intended to, but she had to come up with a good reason to make Casper leave the horse at her ranch.

"That right? Wish I could stay around to see that."

"Yeah, me, too." She all but rolled her eyes.

"Is Black Jack losing weight?"

Stephanie felt an overwhelming desire to do something physical to Casper. Something unpleasant. She took a deep breath. "Not a pound. I hope you didn't forget to roll up your truck windows. I saw that black cat hanging around here this morning."

"Well, damnation!" Casper wheeled and started back to his truck just in time to see a quick black feline jump out of the front seat and dash around the corner of the bunkhouse.

Casper started running and Stephanie began to laugh. She tried to stop herself, but she couldn't. Casper would be apoplectic, and she would only provoke his ire by laughing at him. But damn, it was too funny that he'd fallen prey to Familiar's pungent brand of revenge two days in a row.

"Dammit!" Rupert stood at his open truck door cursing

a blue streak. He grabbed his shotgun from the backseat of the truck. "I'm going to blast that cat into a million pieces."

"Hold on there." Stephanie got a grip on her laughter. "No firearms on the premises, Rupert. I'm serious." She walked to him and put her hand gently on the barrel. "This isn't the place. I'll get you some paper towels."

She trotted to the bunkhouse, returned with a roll of towels and handed them to him. "I can't imagine why that cat persists in doing this. He doesn't bother my vehicles."

"If he gets close enough, I'll run him down."

Stephanie had no worries that Familiar was foolish or careless enough to get in front of Rupert Casper's truck. "I'll take those." She took the dirty wad of paper towels. "And I'll let you know how Black Jack is doing. My best advice is to give me some time. You'll reap the rewards of my efforts—guaranteed."

"Get rid of that damn cat."

"Have a safe trip to Missoula," she said as she walked toward the trash can on the front porch of the bunkhouse. She was laughing softly to herself as Casper drove away.

Sitting here in the window of the bunkhouse, I have a dilemma. I've found something. I was headed out to get Stephanie when that vile biped, Rupert Casper, drove up. That required a priority shift on my part. Messing up his truck became my first goal, and I have to say the man doesn't have sense enough to pour piss out of a boot, pun intended. He left his window down again. Well, duh. When opportunity opens a window, this is one black cat who's going to jump through it.

I have to say, it was a satisfying sideshow. Leather seats. Sometimes vanity makes my job so much easier.

But that's done, and I have to decide whether to bring Miss Cowgirl in here and show her what I've discovered. I knew there was a backstory on Johnny Kreel. My initial computer check came up with evidence to support the story he told Stephanie, but somehow it didn't ring true. At least not to me. Now I discover this cell phone with a series of calls made to Washington, D.C.

What cowboy calls the nation's capital on a regular basis?

So I punched the call button, and a perky young woman answered, "Project Omega." Now my Latin is rusty, but last time I checked, omega is the last letter in the Greek alphabet and means "the end." That's exactly the kind of name the government gives some kind of secret agency.

Maybe it's a stretch, but I think Johnny Kreel is a federal agent of some sort. He showed up just at the right moment. He has a skill set that makes him valuable to Stephanie, so she decided to keep him around. He acts like a law officer when no one is looking, and he has a weapon in his truck that looks police issue. My interpretation—he's an under-cover federal agent here on assignment.

Am I jumping to conclusions?

Not a chance. This is the real deal. Johnny Kreel has been sent to Running Horse Ranch. Now I'm going to figure out why. What I can't decide is whether to alert Miss Cowgirl to this. If she feels that Johnny has betrayed her, she'll send him packing. And that might be the worst thing that could happen. Johnny may be what's standing between her and harm.

Why is someone after Stephanie? Why would they burn down her barn? Thank goodness Johnny was here or some of those horses would have burned to death.

While I don't like keeping this information from Miss

Cowgirl, I'm going to. For the moment. Until I dig up more info on Johnny and Project Omega.

Now, I need sustenance. My brain has furiously burned countless calories as I've puzzled out this situation. Hmm. Stephanie has gone into the kitchen. With a little nudge, I can make her think grilled fish.

There she is, looking through the freezer for food. I'll brush against her leg, get her attention, then pull the old Rasputin number on her. I'll visualize exactly what I want. See it, Miss Cowgirl. Look into my eyes and see: coals dusted with a layer of ash. Salmon sizzling over charcoal. Gaze deeper, Stephanie. Smell that aroma. Wonderful on the crisp air.

"How about some grilled salmon, Familiar? There's some right here."

"Meow."

Humanoids are fairly easy to manipulate in the right circumstances. And they never see it coming.

Chapter Seven

Stephanie put the fish in the sink to thaw. One drawback to living in such isolation was the lack of fresh fish and produce. She relied heavily on frozen foods. But it was a small price to pay for the solitude and beauty of her life.

She rummaged through her cabinets for wild rice and laid out the components for a meal. When Johnny got back, she'd start preparations.

Until then, she needed to work some horses and attend to the many daily chores of the ranch.

As she was about to leave the kitchen, the photograph of her and Rory caught her eye. It was sitting at an odd angle, as if someone had picked it up and put it back.

Rory. How had someone so vital simply disappeared?

She lifted the photo and took it to the kitchen window where the light was good. As she studied the image, she remembered in vivid detail how perfect that week at the beach with Rory had been.

He was such a handsome man—tall and blond, like a Viking god. He'd had the best laugh. That was the first thing that drew her to him. His laughter had been free and generous and easy to ignite.

In many ways, he'd been her polar opposite. That had been a plus, though. He'd offset her seriousness with his lighthearted "Live and let live" humor. He'd balanced her streak of duty and responsibility with a madcap desire for fun. She was a "Play it safe" gal and he was a gambler. The combination had been terrific.

She missed him.

A tear plopped down on the glass surface of the photo and she angrily brushed it away. That time was gone. Rory was gone. The only thing she had was this moment and the life she'd begun to build. That would be enough. She could carry on her grandfather's horse-training methods and make a difference for the animals and people she touched. It wasn't insignificant. The only trouble was that she'd never thought she would be doing it alone.

The black cat rubbed against her leg, and she put the picture back and sat down at the table with Familiar on her lap. "I'm glad you're here," she whispered to him.

Stephanie had a hard time admitting it, but she was lonely. The cat was extraordinary company. And Johnny Kreel had also stepped into a breach. He was a cowboy, a drifter, and soon he'd be down the road. Cowboys were a breed that didn't take to fences or hobbles. Freedom, no matter what the cost, was all that mattered.

But while he was here—

She heard a horse whinny, and she reluctantly put Familiar on the floor. Duty called. Grabbing a light jacket, she headed to the barn and the horses that needed to be worked.

JOHNNY GROUND-TIED CIMARRON, noting that Stephanie had done an excellent job with the mare's training. She stood like a rock. When he'd worked his grandfather's farm in Alabama, he'd become fully aware of how important a well-trained horse was.

Sometimes the horse was the difference between life and death. And most horses, once they understood what was being asked of them, were willing to oblige.

He scrutinized the flatland that lay to the south, placing in his head the location where he and Stephanie had been mending the fence. He was on the ridge above the pasture—the same place where he'd seen the reflection of sun on binoculars.

It wasn't a coincidence that someone was spying on Stephanie the same day her barn burned. This was bad business. The quicker he wrapped it up, the better for everyone. Especially for Stephanie.

As he slowly walked a grid of the area looking for any clues, he hoped the watcher wasn't Rory Sussex. If Rory came back from the dead, as it were, Stephanie would suffer. Carlos Diego was bad enough, but he was a crook and a lowlife. Stephanie would ultimately deal with that.

Rory was her fiancé, the man she'd believed in enough to share her heart. To find out who he really was would be devastating.

Johnny knew that from personal experience, because Rory had been his partner. A man he trusted with his life on delicate international information-gathering missions. More times than he could count, he'd placed his life in Rory's hands, and Rory had always come through for him.

Then things had changed.

Johnny wasn't certain if the money had gotten to Rory, or if Carlos Diego had found a weakness where he could apply leverage and turn Rory. Or if Rory had simply lived too long in the shadows and lost touch with the part of himself that needed light.

A lot of undercover agents ended up throwing in with the bad guys. Johnny had seen plenty of it.

Whatever happened to Rory, it had nearly cost Johnny his life in Colombia, and it had put Stephanie in danger now.

They'd been working a gun-smuggling operation that was headquartered in Colombia but reached all the way to the Middle East. Carlos Diego could supply anything—weapons, drugs, delicate information on U.S. operatives in dangerous countries. And Carlos was always willing to sell to the highest bidder.

The man had no allegiance—to country or anything else. He was a total mercenary. And Rory had spent months worming his way into the Diego organization as a top-notch, take-any-risk pilot. His daring feats had earned Diego's admiration and then his trust.

Rory had been situated in the catbird seat to feed information on Diego's moves to Johnny, who was posing as a wealthy Texas oilman, interested in expanding his revenue stream into the guns and drug trade.

Things had been going perfectly. Until Rory inexplicably fed Johnny some bad information. In his guise as the Texas oilman, Johnny had taken a meeting in Bogotá with one of Diego's right-hand men. The stated goal was an exchange of guns and drugs for cash. Johnny had the cash for delivery, but he'd been met with an ambush. Before he could even offer the money, two machine guns had opened fire. Johnny had barely escaped. He knew someone had blown his cover, and the most logical source was Rory.

Johnny's suspicions had been confirmed when Rory failed to check in at his appointed time. Though agents in

Project Omega operated with almost total autonomy, weekly check-ins were required. Johnny had survived the attempt on his life, and he'd been eager to make sure Rory was still in place. But Rory never called.

At first Johnny had been worried that Rory was actually dead, that Diego had put two and two together and figured Johnny and Rory both for federal plants. While Diego might not know about Project Omega, the high-level group of federal agents from all branches of law enforcement, Diego had to know that the U.S. government was interested in his illegal activities. Diego could easily have killed Rory and left no evidence for anyone to find.

But then there was the mysterious plane crash. Not one scrap of the wreckage was ever found in the impenetrable jungle, even though Johnny had personally conducted a search.

It was possible that Rory had died in the crash, but Johnny didn't believe it for a minute.

When informants began to report sightings of Rory in developing countries, appearing momentarily in one disguise or another, then disappearing again without a trace, it was apparent to Johnny that Rory was on the run. Finally, news had leaked to Johnny from other sources that Rory had betrayed Diego—had in fact intercepted valuable information that could put dozens of U.S. agents and operatives at terrible risk. Word came that Rory was offering the information on the international market to the highest bidder.

And Rory, who had once been his partner and closest friend, was now his quarry.

Johnny had almost cornered Rory twice—once in Afghanistan and once in St. Petersburg—but he'd escaped both times. Rory was a master at self-preservation. He'd done the expedient thing to cover his tracks, even though it had meant leaving Stephanie to fend for herself.

Now Johnny and the Feds were after Rory—and so was Carlos Diego. Diego wasn't the kind of man who let his employees get away with stealing from him. Carlos wouldn't rest until Rory was found and made to pay.

Stephanie Ryan was the perfect bait to close the trap on Rory. Or, even worse, Johnny had come to suspect that Rory had actually hidden the information here at Running Horse Ranch. The barn fire was evidence that Diego had come to the same conclusion. Johnny only hoped that he could use her—and keep her safe from Diego.

As he moved around the rock-strewn ridge, he found the lack of evidence telling. A professional had been watching Stephanie.

Was it Rory or was it one of Diego's men?

In a patch of sand Johnny at last found something. The partial bootprint was a perfect match for the tread of the print Familiar had found at the barn fire. Big print. Big man. It was likely Plenty, a monster of a man with a fondness for giving pain to others.

Johnny thought of Plenty Gonzalez. The stories circulating about the man's brutality made strong people cringe. It was possible the tales had been manufactured to create an aura of dread around the mercenary. It was also possible that every word was true.

One such tale involved a rich South American businessman who'd cheated Diego. The businessman had gone to his elaborate and well-guarded beach home to find pieces of his wife in every room in the house.

Men like Diego and Plenty were capable of anything.

Johnny continued his search of the area, but found

nothing else. Diego's men were watching Running Horse Ranch. His sources were almost as good as the CIA's. Money could, indeed, buy anything.

When Johnny got back to the ranch, he'd find an excuse to drive into town. It was time to place a call to his supervisor. Hance Bevins needed to know about the barn fire. Additional agents had to be dispatched to the area. Things could turn ugly in a flash, and Johnny wanted backup at the ready.

BLACK JACK TROTTED to the paddock fence when Stephanie approached. Her heart lifted at the change in his attitude. Maybe, just maybe, he was really coming around.

She snapped on a lead rope and took him to the barn where she cross-tied him and groomed him again. Horses enjoyed the stroke of a good brush through their hide, and Black Jack was no exception. He preened as she groomed him with the stiff brush.

She put a lightweight saddle on him and let it rest. He'd been ridden before. It wasn't like taking a green horse and teaching him to accept the saddle and bridle. This was, in fact, harder, because Black Jack had been hurt, and she had no clue what he might identify as a source of pain. Some horses locked in on the saddle or bridle as the instrument of pain. Others zeroed in on the human.

But Black Jack gave no objection as she carefully cinched the saddle. Just tight enough that it wouldn't slip if he did something unfortunate. A loose saddle was dangerous—it could slide under the horse or tangle around his back feet and cause serious injury.

Once the saddle was tight, she hesitated. Saddle first. Bridle later. She'd work him and see if the jouncing of the saddle upset him.

They went to the round pen and Black Jack walked out like a perfect gentleman. He took his position by the rail and went to work, walking, trotting, catering and whoaing on command. He worked as if he were the best-behaved horse in the universe, and Stephanie's heart soared at his potential and beauty.

Familiar came out of the bunkhouse and sat beside the round pen watching. For a moment, Stephanie even forgot the barn fire and the nightmare of what could have been lost. She was totally in the moment with Black Jack, her attention absorbed by the work at hand.

She finished the session, stopped him and then asked him to walk toward her. This was a matter of trust. Before, he'd tried to kill her. Now she was putting herself in harm's way, if the stallion chose to attack.

He stopped a foot from her and put his head down for a rub. "You are the best," she whispered as she rubbed his star and scratched behind his ears.

In a split second, his head came up and his nostrils flared. The change was so sudden, so unexpected, that Stephanie didn't react quickly enough. Before she could get out of his way, Black Jack shouldered her to the ground.

He gathered himself and in one mighty leap, cleared the railing of the round pen. Stephanie scrambled to her feet and made a grab for the trailing lunge line, but she missed it by inches.

Black Jack was free and running as hard as he could toward the road.

"Oh, no!" Stephanie ran out of the round pen toward her vehicle. Black Jack was headed straight to danger. She had to stop him.

She was almost at the truck when the first shot sounded.

A bullet hole appeared in the front fender of her truck only inches from where she stood.

She dove to the ground with Familiar beside her.

Peeking around the corner, she tried to find the shooter, but all she could see was Black Jack running like the hounds of hell were after him.

"Meow!" Familiar cried, nudging her toward Johnny's truck and trailer. It was a good plan. If she could get there, she could make it to the house where Rory had stashed some rifles.

She didn't much care for guns, but they were a necessity on a ranch.

As she ran between the trucks, another shot rang out. Familiar stood on both back legs and tried to open the door of Johnny's truck.

"Come on," she said to the cat. "There's no time—"

"Meow!"

The cat was so insistent that she opened the door. Familiar leaped in and rooted Johnny's jacket away from what looked like a high-powered rifle. Beside it was a deadly pistol.

"Holy crap," Stephanie said. "This is an arsenal."

And exactly what she needed.

She grabbed the rifle and took her position behind the vehicle for protection. With the major scope attached, she scanned the horizon. To her utter amazement, she saw a man running. Running hard. And hard on his trail was a furious black stallion.

Black Jack wasn't running away from her. He was chasing the man who'd tried to shoot her.

"Well, I'll be damned," she said, following the action through the scope.

The man leaped into the bed of a dark pickup and the truck churned dirt as it spun away. Black Jack followed for a moment, then circled and headed back to the ranch.

Stephanie saw with some relief that the lunge line had broken and was no longer trailing behind the stallion. She lowered the rifle and waited for the horse to come back in the barnyard. He trotted to the gate of the round pen and stopped, as if waiting for her to resume his work.

"We're done for the day," Stephanie said as she caught hold of his halter and patted his neck. "You are some kind of guy, you know that?" She put her cheek against him, feeling the heat of his exertion.

She knew how remarkable every living creature could be, but this horse had still astounded her. In a matter of days, he'd gone from fearful attacker to bold protector.

. "And I promise. Whatever it takes, I'll keep you safe from Rupert Casper."

Black Jack turned and uttered a soft whinny. He swung his head back and gave Stephanie a nudge. She was caught off balance and nearly fell. When she righted herself, she saw Familiar standing at the door of the bunkhouse, watching her.

The cat was acting strange, but then so was the horse. And so was Rupert Casper. Why would he send men to shoot at her?

"Meow." Familiar now stood at the door of Johnny's truck. She'd left it open when she'd gotten out the rifle. The rifle, and the handgun… Johnny was certainly well armed for a rodeo rider.

And maybe that was what her problems were about, she thought as she walked to the truck. Black Jack might not be at the root of the attacks. Rupert Casper might not be the source of her troubles.

The terrible thing was that Rupert Casper was a known quantity. She could almost predict what he might do. But Johnny—he was a total wild card. If some thugs were after him—thugs willing to burn down a barn with horses in it, much less take a potshot at her—they'd take it as far as necessary to get what they wanted.

But what did they want?

She slammed the truck door and walked into the barn. Johnny had ridden out to the north. She'd track him and get the answers she needed to defend the place and the creatures she loved.

Judging from the expression on Miss Cowgirl's face, she's had an epiphany. After the barn fire and nearly being shot— all within twenty-four hours—she's put it together that Johnny Kreel isn't who he says he is. And it looks like she's going to ride the range to find him and attempt to get the truth.

I so hate riding horses. There's this whole fight-or-flight thing that goes on whenever a horse senses a cat on its back. Even a domestic cat. I mean, even though I was raised in an alley, my mother and I never ate horse. While we were often hungry, we had standards. Equine was not on the menu, though more than a few times I've sampled the delicacies of rat. Properly prepared… No, not even the glaze of memory and the efforts of my beloved mother can put a happy patina on those days of desperation. Rat is not tasty, no matter how well prepared. And living in an alley, we had no way to prepare anything.

My life with Eleanor and Peter, my adopted humanoid parents, is paradise. I only wish my mother had lived to share it with me.

My, my. My mood is certainly melancholy. Must be the

thought of climbing up on that horse. But there's no getting around that. I'm not about to let Miss Cowgirl take off across the flatlands on her own. She needs my noble protection, though I must admit that Black Jack performed ably. Who would have thought that devil would care about Stephanie? Just goes to show that his heart isn't totally hardened.

Here she comes, leading Flicker. At least this is one of the shorter horses. Not so far to the ground, should something go wrong. And she seems to be a tractable little horse, ready to jog along at a steady pace without any of the galloping and bucking stuff.

I have to convince Stephanie to take me. She's going to resist. That's the biped way—to say no. It's a defense mechanism, I think. Humanoids have never been able to decide if they're fight-or-flight creatures. They take one course of action, then the other, then double back. They're bipolar when it comes to matters of survival. Which is why they meet each new situation with one attitude—no.

But I'll wear her down. And I'll be on the back of that saddle when she rides after Johnny. It's in my job description.

Chapter Eight

Johnny was almost back to the ranch when he heard gunshots. His legs tightened on Cimarron, and she leaped forward at a dead gallop. As they rode hard for home, his fingers found the small handgun he kept strapped to his ankle. He'd left his more powerful weapons in his truck, but he always carried some form of protection.

He tore into the barnyard just as Stephanie, with Familiar riding shotgun, came trotting past the corral on Flicker. Her first expression at seeing him was relief, but it quickly turned to suspicion and anger.

The cat, so to speak, was out of the bag. Somehow, Stephanie had gotten wind that he wasn't who he'd said he was.

Watching her expression, he tried to determine how betrayed she felt.

His first impulse was to explain, but he didn't. He dismounted, walked Cimarron beside his truck and began to untack her. Stephanie's saddles had burned in the barn fire, but Johnny always carried two or three with him. He stowed the gear in the tack compartment of the trailer, working silently, waiting for her to start the conversation.

"Who the hell *are* you?" she finally asked.

Even Familiar glared at him. The cat had jumped from the back of the saddle onto the hood of his truck.

"What happened here?" He ignored her question and pointed at the bullet hole in his truck.

"Someone shot at me when I was working Black Jack." Stephanie hurled the words at him. "The horse could have been killed."

"Or you could have." Johnny removed Cimarron's bridle and slipped a halter on her.

"Either or both of us. And I don't think it's Rupert Casper doing the shooting."

He didn't acknowledge or deny her statement. He had to find out what she knew before he admitted to anything.

"Now I'm going to ask you one more time, and if I don't get a straight answer, you're going to pack up and get off my property." She paused only a second, and when she spoke, her voice was harsh. "Who the hell *are* you?"

"I'm a federal agent." He watched the impact of his words. They were like slaps. Her face reddened and he could see her temper rising.

"A federal agent posing as a horse trainer?" She shook her head. "That's rich. You must really take me for a fool."

He reached into his back pocket, brought out his badge holder and tossed it to her.

She flipped it open, her expression going slack. "This says you're a federal law officer, but it doesn't say with which agency."

He nodded. "I don't work for an agency. I work for a project. And that's all I can tell you."

"What are you doing here at my ranch?"

That was the tricky part. He wanted to come clean and just tell her about Rory. But too much, too fast would alienate her.

"Rory Sussex was my partner."

He stepped forward and caught her elbow when she looked as if she might fall to the ground. "Come on off the horse." He eased her down, and she made no protest. As he waited for her to ask questions, he removed Flicker's saddle and turned the little mare loose in a pasture.

When he finished, Stephanie had regained her equilibrium. "You knew Rory? You've been here for two days, and you never mentioned that you knew my dead fiancé."

He sighed. "I couldn't. I shouldn't have now. But there are some things you need to know if you're going to survive this. The people who burned the barn and shot at you—they think Rory stole something from them. They're here to reclaim it."

"And why are you here?"

He hesitated. "The U.S. government wants it, too. But I'm also here to look out for you."

"Right. You promised Rory, didn't you?" Her tone was rife with sarcasm.

"No, I didn't promise Rory. We were partners, but in the last year, we'd grown apart. Before he… I'd begun to suspect that Rory was playing both sides against each other. Then he disappeared and now you're in a bad situation. I'm afraid there are people who believe Rory hid something here at the ranch. Something valuable. Someone needs to help you."

"Well, you can take your magnanimous butt, put it in the seat of your truck and drive yourself right off this property. Now. I wasn't in any danger until you showed up. All of this has to do with you, not me. Rory didn't give me anything that anyone would want. Just some memories and a few dreams, obviously all of which were lies." Her voice thickened and she wiped at her eyes. "Get off my ranch." She wheeled and stalked off toward the house.

The black cat cast a green glare at him before he, too, left, hurrying after Stephanie.

That certainly went well, Johnny silently berated himself. He'd bungled the job. Instead of leaving, though, he examined the bullet hole in his truck. High-powered rifle shot. If it had hit Stephanie, it would have killed her.

He prepared to feed the stock their evening meal and bided his time.

He couldn't leave Stephanie, no matter how mad it made her. Maybe she was right. Maybe the trouble had followed him there. That thought was disconcerting, to say the least.

But, ultimately, Carlos Diego would have found Stephanie. Diego would leave no stone unturned in his efforts to track down the information that had gone missing at the same time Rory's plane supposedly crashed.

That Rory had somehow hidden a disk or coded document here at the ranch was a pretty logical assumption. It was exactly the same conclusion that Johnny had come to, which was why he, too, was here at Running Horse Ranch.

The problem was that his primary concern was no longer recovering the information. He'd come to care about Stephanie and her work. Protecting her had superseded retrieving the government secrets—at least in his mind. And that was a dangerous place for an undercover agent to find himself.

The one rule he'd never broken in his career as an intelligence agent was to keep himself from getting personally involved in any case. Once the emotions engaged, the brain slowed.

Yet he couldn't help himself. In a very short time, Stephanie had penetrated his emotional defenses. She'd won him over with her simple caring for the creatures around her, with her passion for her work and her desire to make things better.

He wasn't about to leave her alone to face Carlos Diego and Plenty.

STEPHANIE POURED A SHOT of bourbon over ice and took a sip. She wasn't a big drinker, but the bomb Johnny had dropped on her required some fortification. Bourbon was the best remedy in the house to stop her shaking knees.

She took another sip, concentrating on the burn of the liquor as it hit her gut. Too much on an empty stomach and she'd be dog sick on top of everything else.

She went to the sink where the fish she'd put out for supper had thawed. Her first temptation was to throw it in the trash. Where had her mind been, planning out menus for Johnny Kreel?

A federal agent! For an organization so secretive it didn't have a name. Right. What kind of fool did Johnny take her for? If *Johnny* was even his name.

She slammed the fish into a pan and stirred up a marinade. At least she and Familiar would enjoy the salmon. Johnny could eat buffalo chips for all she cared.

Glancing out the window, she saw him hauling feed to the horses, as if nothing had happened. Well, he was an idiot if he thought he was staying at her place another night. He could feed the horses and mend fences until the cows came home, but he was leaving.

She thought about Tex. The gelding's leg was finally getting better. Hauling him off in a horse trailer now would undo all the good that had been done by cold water hosing and anti-inflammatory medicine.

It wasn't Tex's fault that he belonged to a bad man—a liar, a cheat and a betrayer.

She put the rice on to cook and walked out the back to start the grill. Johnny wouldn't change her plans or her routine. Once he was gone, the steady rhythm of her life would pick up again.

Off in the distance, she heard the howl of a wolf. The wild creatures came close at night, but in the past they hadn't bothered her or the horses. Until the barn had burned, she'd had protection and shelter for all the live-stock. Now many of them were out in paddocks. It made her nervous, but there was nothing she could do about it.

Tomorrow, she'd find a contractor and start the rebuild-ing process—and hope the insurance company paid up to cover the cost of a new barn. Her credit was good. She'd tackle the problem that way.

Her thoughts were on her dismal financial situation when she saw the twin beams of a car's headlights in the blue dusk. Someone was out by the western boundary of her property, watching. And that someone wanted her to know he was watching.

Goosebumps danced along her skin. These men were brazen. They'd been close enough to slip into the house and hurt her, yet they'd chosen to burn a barn. A warning? A threat? Most likely both.

What had Rory taken that was worth so much? Rory had always had abundant cash. She'd never thought to question his affluence. He was a pilot. Flyboys made good money. That had been her assumption.

Wrong. So wrong. But if Rory had stashed this valuable information at Running Horse Ranch, where might it be?

Once that question popped into her head, she couldn't

let it go. She set the charcoal ablaze and retreated into the house. With Familiar at her heels, she went to the bedroom and retrieved the ornate wooden box where she'd kept each of Rory's letters.

She'd met him while on a visit to the Alabama beaches at Gulf Shores. After five years working at an advertising agency in New Orleans, she'd been toying with the idea of going to law school and working to protect animals' rights. She'd met a member of the Animal Legal Defense Fund, a group of attorneys, animal lovers and environmentalists dedicated to helping write better anticruelty laws and assisting local law enforcement agencies in all fifty states to prosecute animal abuse cases. At that point, she'd been considering a change of career.

So many places used animals for entertainment or pleasure—without ever considering the needs of the living creatures involved.

Working with a group like ALDF seemed like a job made in heaven. But once she met Rory, he'd resurrected her dream of helping horses using her grandfather's kind and gentle techniques.

Rory had had the money to buy the land in South Dakota. He'd paid to build the barns and restore the old cabin, giving it modern plumbing, wiring and conveniences.

Never in a million years would she ever have suspected that Rory wasn't the gung-ho, animal-loving pilot he made himself out to be. He'd had his own small fleet of planes—she'd seen them. And she'd seen his work-order sheets, ferrying humans and freight from his base in New Orleans to points in Central and South America and up the Eastern Seaboard. He'd made money—a staggering amount, at least to her.

And none of it was real.

She put the box of letters beside the bed. She would read through each one, see if she could find a hint or clue as to what Rory had been up to. He'd only been to Running Horse Ranch a dozen times in the months before he disappeared, making quick trips between his business obligations. Most of the details of setting up the ranch he'd left to her. Looking back, it seemed strange to her that he'd been at the ranch just two days before the plane crash.

The day he died, he'd supposedly been wrapping up loose ends in his transport business in preparation for the move to South Dakota. He'd claimed it was his last week of work.

Had he left something on the ranch premises during his last trip?

She returned to the kitchen. As she prepared the fish for the grill, she squeezed her eyes shut, trying to block out the image of Rory on the beach, his Hawaiian shirt open to reveal his muscled chest, his blue eyes crinkled in laughter and his white teeth flashing. He'd been like a movie star dropped down into her path.

And he'd shared her dream. He'd touched the most secretive part of her spirit and made her believe that he knew it and understood.

All of it had been a lie.

She found her fingers gripping the pan of fish tightly, and it took all of her effort not to fling it against a wall.

The black cat brushed against her ankles, and she finally won the battle of self-control. Rory Sussex and his lies had hurt her, but he would not win.

She bent to stoke the cat, pulling Familiar into her arms. He licked her chin and head-butted her, letting her know he shared her grief.

"Rory didn't just die," she whispered to the cat. "He killed a dream with his lies." For the first time, she seriously doubted that she could make a go of Running Horse Ranch. "Maybe I should sell out."

Familiar put a black paw on her lips, as if telling her not to speak. He shook his head slowly.

"I don't believe you." She kissed the top of his head. "You do understand. Far more than any human does." She put him down and picked up the fish. "Let's get this cooked and get back in the house."

Night had fallen, and the lights of the vehicle she'd seen earlier were gone. Or at least they'd been turned off. As the fish grilled, she looked out at her spread. The windows in the bunkhouse shone brightly in the black night. Johnny hadn't left. Obviously, he had no intention of leaving.

In the morning, she'd put him on the road. That would give Tex another night to heal. Besides, driving the winding, uneven roads at night was an unnecessary danger, even for a liar.

Using tongs, she picked up the salmon and went back inside. The rice had cooked, and she'd prepared an asparagus salad. She made a plate for Familiar and one for herself.

"This isn't so bad," she said to the cat. "We're a team now, Familiar. Just the two of us."

As she was lifting a forkful of the succulent fish to her mouth, a knock sounded at the door. Sighing, she lowered her fork and went to answer it. Familiar, she noticed, wasn't going to be dislodged from his plate. He'd consumed half his salmon and was working diligently on the other half.

Johnny stood in the doorway, filling the frame with his broad shoulders and lean body. "Someone's riding the perimeter of the property," he said. "I'm going to check it out."

Stephanie hesitated. "Don't."

He arched an eyebrow, waiting.

"If they draw you out there, they'll come in here and burn something else." It was hard to admit, but the fact that Johnny was on the premises felt like a safeguard.

"You think my staying here will deter them? If they want to burn, they'll come whether I'm here or not." Frustration was clear in his voice. "I've tried to call for backup, but I can't raise my superior. There's no reception at all."

"Lovely. Maybe if the agency had a name, you might have a superior who answered the phone."

He grasped her shoulders firmly. "I don't blame you for being angry. I don't blame you for hating me. But don't for one second think this is a situation that you can gloss over with sarcasm. Those men will hurt you. They will torture you if they think you can tell them where Rory hid the—"

"The what?"

"I don't know what he had."

"You don't know?" She couldn't keep the sarcasm from her tone. It was preposterous that Johnny didn't know what he was looking for.

"We didn't know Rory had turned. Not for sure." He averted his eyes. "I suspected, but I didn't believe it. Once we couldn't find a trace of his plane… I had to acknowledge my suspicions."

"Suspicions of Rory or suspicions that he didn't crash?" Stephanie could barely speak. The full breadth of Rory's lies came sharply into focus. She saw it on Johnny's face, though he recovered quickly.

"Rory isn't dead, is he?" she pressed.

Johnny started to turn from her but she grabbed his shirt

and spun him back to face her. "Tell me the truth, you coward. Rory is alive, isn't he?"

"We don't know." Johnny held her gaze.

Her heart squeezed painfully. Of all the betrayals, lying about being dead had to be the worst. She could accept that Rory was a scoundrel, but not that kind of liar. Not to her. All he had to do was tell her he was moving on. She'd never have pursued the issue, never have known about his secret life or web of lies. And he knew that.

She read the pity on Johnny's face, and it was more of an answer than anything he could have said out loud. "You think Rory is behind the barn fire, don't you?"

Johnny took a deep breath.

"Answer me." She'd never felt such fury. She could feel her body trembling.

"I don't know."

She drew back and slapped Johnny with all her strength. She hadn't expected to strike out, but the idea that Johnny had come to the ranch, lying through his teeth, pretending to be some cowboy with an injured horse so he could sneak around and spy on her, was more than she could take.

In truth, she wanted to hit Rory, to land a blow so powerful that he would drop at her feet. Rory wasn't there, but Johnny was. And he would do just fine as the target of her hurt and wrath.

She drew back to slap him again, but Johnny caught her arm. In one swift movement, he spun her around and brought her against his chest, his arms wrapping around her, holding her tight as she struggled.

Fury made tears come to her eyes. She tried to bite and claw, to kick and savage him in any way she could, but Johnny held her tightly. He made no effort to calm her, but he held on until the full tide of her anger had washed away, leaving her depleted and embarrassed.

He gently let her go. When he no longer held her, she sank to the arm of the nearby sofa. "I hate you both," she said.

"I don't blame you. You didn't deserve this."

She turned away, noting that Familiar was standing in the doorway, watching to be sure she wasn't hurt. She came to a decision.

"Tomorrow, I'm going to pack up the horses and leave here. I'll move them down to a friend's place in Oklahoma. If there's anything hidden here at Running Horse Ranch, you can have it, or they can have it. Or if Rory is still alive and he wants it, then he can come and get it. I never want to hear his name again."

"It's not going to be that simple," Johnny said softly. "Carlos Diego will never believe that you don't know something."

The full impact of the web she'd become caught in dawned on Stephanie. "You're saying I can't get out of this."

Johnny nodded. "Not now. Not until we either find Rory or find what he took from Diego."

"Ask Diego," Stephanie said.

"If it were that simple, it would have been done already. We're going to have to find it, if it's here."

"Just the two of us?"

He pointed to the cat. "The three of us. And we need to get busy now."

Chapter Nine

Stephanie walked into the kitchen. She needed a moment to pull herself together. The food was still on the table, but she'd lost her appetite. Her stomach was knotted, and fear constricted her throat. The people watching her meant business. They had no qualms about killing.

"Do you have any weapons?" Johnny asked.

She nodded. "Rory kept some rifles in the linen closet." She retrieved the two big rifles, noting that Johnny handled them with expertise. No big surprise there, as she'd come to discover. The gentle horse trainer had a very dark side.

"These are good," he said, as he made sure the weapons were ready for use. "This one has a nightscope." He arranged them for easy access, putting the ammunition she brought out near at hand.

It was odd that she'd never noticed or even thought about the implications of such weapons in the house. Rory had simply put the guns in the closet without comment. She'd never cared for firearms, but she hadn't questioned him about the stash of weapons. Rory wasn't a hunter, had never shown the least interest in killing animals for sport. That would have been a deal breaker for her. It had never crossed her mind that the weapons he kept were used to hunt humans.

There were many questions she'd failed to put on the table, but what normal person would think to ask, "Hey, do you happen to have a double identity?"

She pushed her despair aside and focused on the immediate problem. "Do you think they'll attack tonight?" she asked. She tried to keep her voice steady.

"It's hard to tell," he said. "A lot depends on what Diego thinks is here."

"Stop this hedging! Johnny, tell me the truth." Stephanie was sick of the lies and half-truths.

"I can't."

"What if something happens to you? What if they hurt you and I'm left here alone? I deserve a chance to defend myself, but I can't if I don't know what this is about."

"If you knew the full story, you could be in even greater danger." Johnny went to all the windows, drawing the curtains together.

She wanted to shake the facts out of him. "Did Rory betray his country?"

Johnny stopped. "I don't know, Stephanie."

"Don't know or won't tell?"

"I'll tell you everything I can."

"Which amounts to nothing." She turned away in disgust. How in the world had she become embroiled in such a mess? Her only crime had been to fall in love with a man who pretended to be a charming flyboy, a man who enjoyed the idea of a simple life working with horses. She'd never wanted riches or wealth; none of that meant anything to her. She didn't know what the men lurking outside the ranch wanted—why they were willing to kill her.

"I'm doing what I think is best to protect you," Johnny said.

"Call for help. Surely you have some fallback way of communicating with your people."

His shoulders sagged for a split second. "I tried," he said. "I have an emergency radio, but the signal is being blocked."

She knew what that meant. She and Johnny were on their own. If the men outside used the cover of darkness to attack, she and Johnny and Familiar would have to defend themselves as best they could. It was going to be a very long night.

"Since you're here, you might as well eat," she said at last. She hadn't given up on finding the truth, but a head-to-head with Johnny was only going to result in headaches for both of them. She pointed to a seat at the table and set a place for him.

Johnny ate with gratitude and intensity. She toyed with the food on her plate, watching Familiar groom himself in contentment. The cat's appetite hadn't been thrown off at all by the recent events. He'd devoured at least eight ounces of salmon and now looked ready for a nap.

Johnny cleared his throat. "Was there any place on the ranch Rory showed a preference for?"

At his question, she was flooded with memories. Rory had spent time in the bunkhouse, one of the original buildings on the premises he'd worked to modernize. He'd been so proud of his ability to wire the place, bringing in electric heaters to supplement the fireplace, preparing for the day when they'd be able to afford to hire a couple of hands to help with the work.

Rory had also ridden the range often—and alone. He'd come in from a long ride, eager to talk about the wildlife he'd seen and the magnificence of the wilderness right outside his back door, but he'd seldom been specific about where he'd gone or why. At the time, she'd given it no thought. Now it seemed sinister.

There was also the pump house, where he'd fiddled with the mechanics of the well for hours on end. And the tractor shed. And the house, which also bore the stamp of his labor. He'd put in modern appliances and a butane generator that ran both the air-conditioning and the well. Rory had been handy around the ranch, no doubt about it.

"When he was here, he stayed busy working on things." She listed the areas. "I can't say he seemed more interested in one place than another."

Johnny scooted back his chair and walked to the kitchen window. "The lights are still gone."

"Do you think they left?" she asked, hope suddenly springing into her heart. Maybe Carlos Diego's men would simply leave them alone.

"They haven't left," Johnny said. "They won't come at us again tonight. They're regrouping, planning."

"When will they come?"

"A day or two. Maybe a little longer. They have time on their side."

"Aren't they afraid we'll destroy whatever it is they think I have?"

"Good question, which tells me that it's something our government would also want. They're counting on my protecting whatever it is."

She stood and refilled Johnny's tea glass. "What was Diego into?" She thought of novels she'd read, which provided her only frame of reference for this world of criminals. "Drugs? Prostitution? International money laundering?"

"All of the above. Add gunrunning to the list. All sideline businesses—his primary focus is selling information."

"What kind of information?" Stephanie didn't like the sound of this at all. Such were the ingredients for movies—and in the movies a whole lot of stuff got burned, blown up and destroyed, including people.

Johnny finally met her gaze head-on. "The United States has operatives all over the world. Most of them gather information—intelligence. These operatives don't take action. It isn't like James Bond, for the most part. The agents merely keep a finger on the pulse of certain activities in other countries. To negotiate with some countries we rely on information about their activities."

"Activities that have an impact on our country," she said.

"That's right."

"And Rory was an operative?"

"Rory was the exception to the rule. He gathered intelligence, but he also took part in illegal activities as part of his cover. He'd been successfully planted inside the Diego organization. We'd spent years building his cover, his transport business, his personality, his past." Johnny picked up his plate and walked to the sink.

She could tell that he didn't want to talk about this, but she wanted answers—she needed answers. "You owe me an explanation, at least."

He turned slowly, the plate still in his hand. "No, I don't. I'll tell you what I can, Stephanie, because I recognize that you've been wronged. You're caught up in something and you're totally innocent. But there are other lives at stake here—not just yours and mine."

"Then it seems that someone should be checking on us. That someone in power would make sure my barn wasn't torched. Tell me how that happened. My horses could have died. I could have been shot this afternoon. Where is this wonderful organization you work for?"

She saw him swallow and knew he was as worried as she was. That didn't calm her one bit.

She went to the bedroom and brought the box of letters Rory had written her. Once, she'd cherished them. Now the very idea that she'd believed a single word made her feel stupid.

"There may be a clue in these," she said, putting the box in front of Johnny's place at the table. She went to the sink and ran hot water.

While she washed the dishes, Johnny read the letters. Familiar sat beside him, almost as if he, too, were reading along.

Stephanie couldn't help but remember the letters. Some of them included personal references, endearments, dreams. She and Rory had spun out the plans for the ranch and their lives in loving detail.

"He meant to move here and live with you. I believe he was sincere in that."

She froze. She could feel Johnny's gaze on her back, drilling into her. She didn't face him, though. She was struggling to rein in her emotions.

"What does it matter what he intended?" she finally asked. "He lied about everything. Had he come here, it would only be worse for me now."

She heard Johnny's footsteps and then felt his hands grasping her shoulders. His grip was warm and firm, and he held her as he spoke. "He may have lied to you, but I know he loved you."

"He loved me so much he let me create an image of who he was in my head—"

"And he wanted to be that man, Stephanie. You made him want to be the man you thought he was. It's obvious Rory was planning on leaving the agency and building a life with you."

She spun, suddenly furious. "Why are you taking his side? What's he done? Sold the names of his friends to a foreign government? How can you even pretend that there's one single thing about him that's decent?"

Johnny sighed. "Because I know what it feels like to be in a life that requires lies and fabrications to protect the ones you love." The last phrase was spoken softly.

Stephanie saw the sadness in Johnny's eyes. It had never occurred to her that perhaps he, too, had lied his way into a woman's heart.

"Don't defend him. And don't defend yourself. You choose to live a life of lies. You shouldn't drag innocent people in behind you."

His hands dropped to his sides. "You're right." He went to the table and picked up his hat. Slowly he put it on and moved to the back door. "I'll check on the horses before I go to bed."

Stephanie lifted her jacket from the hook by the door. "I'm going, too. I refuse to live like a captive in my own home." As she reached for the doorknob, she felt a sharp pain in the back of her thigh.

Looking back, she found Familiar digging his claws into her leg. "Cat!" She reached back to swat at him, but he dropped lower, wrapping around her calf. His claws dug in deep enough for a firm hold.

"Dammit!" She hopped around the kitchen.

"Even the cat has sense enough to know you shouldn't go outside tonight," Johnny said.

When she heard the hint of amusement in his voice, it was almost her undoing. "Leave me alone. Both of you."

As soon as she turned toward the hallway and her bedroom, Familiar dropped down to the floor. He rubbed against her shin, purring as if he were an angel.

"Traitor," she said as she stalked past him.

JOHNNY EYED THE BLACK CAT. Whatever doubts he'd once harbored about Familiar's abilities he had set aside in the last few days. The cat was a creature of exceptional intelligence, and he could get away with things that would get a human shot.

"Good work, Familiar." He stroked the cat's sleek hide.

When Johnny opened the door to go outside, the cat darted in front of him. Well, it wouldn't hurt to have the feline on guard patrol. The cat had an uncanny awareness of danger.

Johnny was a strong believer in the abilities of all animals to pick up and recognize impulses that were far too subtle for the average human. There were some men and women with a so-called sixth sense. Rory had been one of them. He'd been able to work within a highly volatile crime organization, staying one step ahead of Carlos Diego.

He'd been so successful at it, in fact, that he'd betrayed not only Carlos but the Omega Project.

Johnny slipped through the night, moving silently from paddock to corral to the nearest pasture where Stephanie had put most of the horses.

In the faint glimmer of a new moon, he could see them grazing peacefully. Familiar walked the rail fence, his nose up and his tail straight in the air. He, too, was taking the measure of the night.

Far in the distance a coyote howled, a sound so lonesome that it touched Johnny down in his bones. Rory had nicknamed him "the coyote." It had started as a joke, but the name had stuck. It suited him. Because he never dated, never pursued any of the women who made it clear they'd be interested in a night on the town or a bit more.

Because Johnny had never felt comfortable dragging an innocent person into the web of lies that had become his life. He'd feared what would happen, and now he could see firsthand that he'd been right. Stephanie was living proof.

But the worst of it was that he'd begun to have serious feelings for her.

And that was counterproductive for her and for him.

In coming to the ranch, pretending to be a cowboy on the move, he'd lied to and betrayed her. On top of that, he'd had to deliver the news that Rory was likely alive and had put her in a position of great danger. No, there was no recovering from all of this.

Yet he couldn't ignore his feelings. It had taken all his restraint not to gather her into his arms and hold her, offer the comfort he knew she needed. But that would be a lie on top of a mountain of falsehoods. He couldn't protect her. Hell, he didn't know if they'd survive the week.

The most disturbing part was the fact that he'd been cut off from the rest of the organization. Anything could have happened in the world at large, and none of the news would have filtered to Running Horse Ranch.

When he finished checking all the horses, he stopped by the bunkhouse and got his gear. Stephanie wasn't going to like it, but he intended to spend the night in the main house. It would be easier to keep her safe that way.

He and the cat moved silently through the night, slipping in the back door of the house, which he locked. He closed all the shutters and headed for the sofa. If by some chance Stephanie had fallen asleep, he wasn't going to make noise.

Maybe in the morning things would look better. Stephanie had plans to move the horses to safety, but he knew that would never happen. Carlos wouldn't allow her to leave. But Johnny would cross that bridge when he had to. For the moment, he needed sleep.

WELL, IN TYPICAL *humanoid fashion, things have spiraled out of control in a big-time kind of way. Why is it that bipeds complicate their lives by lying? Felines, a naturally superior species, never lie. We are exactly what you see— perfect creations that come with self-confidence, remarkable balance and agility, a loving nature and a need to control our environments. Not to mention a healthy and finicky appetite.*

I can see that Johnny has developed feelings for Miss Cowgirl. And she likes him back. That's why his betrayal is all the more bitter for her to swallow. Now two felines would simply sniff, romp a bit and then get down to the business of mutual attraction. Not the bipeds. They make everything difficult. So in a time of great danger, Johnny is on the sofa and Miss Cowgirl is locked in her room.

What a mess.

The only positive news around here is that while I was out with Johnny, I didn't sense any other humans around. The horses, also keen observers of human nature, were serene and grazing. I think for tonight, at least, we can settle in for some sleep. Which is a good thing, because I need my beauty rest.

Tomorrow we'll search for whatever Rory stole. If it's here, we'll find it. Once we know what it is, we'll have a better idea of how to proceed.

Chapter Ten

Stephanie awakened to the smell of freshly brewed coffee and cooking bacon. For a moment she snuggled beneath the covers and drifted into half sleep, a place where she felt safe and loved. In the background she could hear her grandfather chanting softly as he made the breakfast that would start their day. She burrowed deeper into the warm quilts and drifted back in time to a morning of sunshine and the joy of learning "the way of the horse" with the slender Oglala elder, her beloved grandfather, who'd never raised his voice in anger.

Her grandfather had just received a blue roan, a beautiful mare who was so head-shy no one could get a halter on her. This was to be the day's lesson—to teach Purple Sage, the horse, to learn to trust her. Stephanie was eager to show her grandfather how hard she'd studied his teachings. She would show Purple Sage that humans could be kind and helpful as well as cruel and abusive.

The smell of cooking bacon teased Stephanie's senses, drawing her toward wakefulness. She was hungry. The day was starting and life was—

She sat up and threw back the covers with a start. She

was a grown woman and her grandfather had been dead for years. The only person who could be cooking was Johnny Kreel. She flung herself out of bed and pulled on jeans and a warm shirt. The mornings were getting colder, and she found clean socks and her boots.

She checked the bedside clock—it was just after daybreak. She had too much to do to waste a minute. Her plan was to load the horse trailer and move some of the horses to a safer location. It would take several trips to transport them all, but once that was done, then she'd decide whether she would stay and fight—or flee.

When she walked into the kitchen, she paused. Johnny, unaware that she was in the room, stood at the stove, turning the bacon in a sizzling skillet. He hummed an old cowboy tune softly under his breath. Familiar sat on a chair at the table, watching. The scene was so homey she felt a catch in her chest. Looking at Johnny work, she had to admit certain things, if only to herself.

Johnny Kreel moved her. He touched something primal and feminine deep inside her. His flannel shirt clung to his broad shoulders, and his worn jeans hugged his lean hips. Every move he made was fluid grace. His whipcord body implied prowess and power, but he'd never used his physicality in a negative way. At least not that she'd ever seen.

Despite herself, she imagined what it would feel like if he wrapped his arms around her and held her. If he kissed her. Would he be a tender and fiery lover? She swallowed, desperately trying to get control of her thoughts. Johnny worked on her, but she couldn't afford to let him. He wasn't to be trusted, and surely she'd learned that bitter lesson from Rory. Or she should have.

But Johnny wasn't Rory, she argued with herself. Rory

had set out to deceive her. Johnny had come along to try to clean up the mess Rory had made. In a way, he was as much a victim in this situation as she was. Rory had put them both between a rock and a hard place.

No matter how mad she was at Johnny's deception, she couldn't deny the attraction she felt. He was a handsome man who embodied so many qualities she admired—and some she couldn't tolerate.

And those were the ones she had to concentrate on if she didn't want to suffer another heartbreak.

He sensed her presence and turned to face her, the spatula in one hand. "Morning." He offered a slightly crooked grin. "Breakfast will be ready in two shakes of a lamb's tail."

She nodded, dropping her gaze, hoping he hadn't picked up on her thoughts. Her emotions were too volatile, and she wasn't sure how much of her inner turmoil might show in her face.

"I hope you don't mind that I took the liberty of starting breakfast," he said.

"No." She went to the coffeepot and poured a cup, taking her time as she tried to figure out how to handle the situation that had been thrust upon her.

Johnny drained the crisp bacon on paper towels and turned to the refrigerator for eggs. "Familiar has ordered two eggs, over easy. What about you?"

Stephanie eyed the cat. "I figured Familiar more for the poached egg kind of cat."

"That was his first choice, but I'm not much into poaching. Fried or scrambled were his choices."

She put her coffee on the counter and retrieved a loaf of bread. "Over easy," she said as she put four slices in the toaster.

Familiar looked from her to Johnny and back to her. He seemed to be assessing the situation. When Johnny put a plate of bacon and eggs in front of him, the cat immediately ate. Stephanie envied him such a ferocious appetite. Something about Johnny made it difficult to eat in his presence. At least for her.

She buttered the toast and found the homemade jam she'd bought in Custer. A local church group had picked blackberries earlier in the season and made the preserves. The taste reminded her of childhood and of making blackberry jam with her grandmother, Olga. Those has been rare moments spent indoors. Given the chance, she was always outside with Running Horse, caring for the stock and watching him train. But she had some treasured memories of her grandmother, too.

"You're thinking about the past, aren't you?" Johnny asked.

Embarrassment crept into her cheeks. "How did you know?"

He shrugged one shoulder as he put a plate of eggs, bacon and toast in front of her. "The left side of your mouth sort of tugs up. It happens whenever you talk about your grandfather, so I figured you were thinking about him."

"Yes," she said, feeling even more exposed. She had to be careful; Johnny could read her like a book.

"I wish I could have met your grandfather," Johnny said, turning from the stove with another plate of hot food in his hand.

He sounded so sincere that she looked at him. She stopped, her fork in midair, and met his gaze. For one long moment they were frozen in that pose. She stared over her fork into his eyes while he held a spatula in one hand and a plate in the other and stood halfway between the stove and the table.

It was craziness, but she felt the blood rush through her body. She had the sense of falling, as if the world had tilted too suddenly and she was going to be flung into space.

In slow motion, Johnny put the plate on the table and lowered the spatula, placing it carefully beside his plate. He came toward her, never breaking the gaze that held them like a magic spell.

She found herself rising from her chair, pushing it away with the backs of her knees. It fell with a loud crash, but she didn't hear it. She was aware that Familiar had stopped eating and was watching them with wide green eyes, but there was no sound in the depth of the moment. There was only Johnny.

Johnny's arms encircled her and she stepped into him, felt his hard chest beneath her fingers and face. This was not smart, and she knew it, but she could no more stop herself than she could fly.

A fire had been smoldering between them from the first moment they'd met, and now it had flamed into life.

She lifted her face and met his lips. His arms pulled her against him and he leaned into the kiss, demanding now instead of receiving.

Stephanie kissed him, pressing into him, yielding and taking the initiative as her body burned to take matters further. The past and future receded. There was only this single moment and the way that Johnny's lips claimed her.

Locked together in a passionate embrace, Stephanie let go of whatever troubles waited outside the cabin. In the passion of the kiss, they didn't exist. She lost herself in the taste and smell and touch of Johnny Kreel. And she never wanted to surface.

Suddenly, Johnny released her. He stepped back as if he'd been scalded, a look of distress on his face.

"What?" she asked.

"The cat." He reached back, swatting at his backside.

Stephanie finally saw the cat. Familiar had dug his claws into Johnny's pants—and likely a good bit of his skin. He hung from Johnny's butt.

"Familiar." She reached for him, but the cat sprang away. He went back to his food and began eating as if nothing had happened.

"I don't think the cat cares for romance in the kitchen," Johnny said, rubbing his backside.

"Familiar is a cat of distinctive likes and dislikes." She brushed imaginary hair out of her eyes. She felt young and green and shy, and the thought of meeting Johnny's penetrating gaze was difficult. Now that the passion had cooled slightly, she was stunned at her own behavior. Never in her life, not even with Rory, had she been so carried away with desire.

Johnny reached across the table and lifted her chin. "Familiar may not approve, but I do."

Again the feeling that her balance was gone washed over her and she put her hands on the table. "Maybe Familiar is right."

Johnny cocked an eyebrow. "Maybe he is. Or maybe he's not. I've wanted to kiss you from the first minute I laid eyes on you. I don't regret it. And I hope you don't."

"This doesn't make sense to me. I'm kissing you, but I don't trust you." She threw up her hands. "I must be completely nuts."

Johnny took his seat at the table. "Look, Stephanie, this is a bad situation, I agree. And if you want to call a halt to it until we've figured out how to deal with Diego, I understand. But as soon as this is over, I intend to pick up exactly where we left off."

"Me-ow." Familiar jumped onto the table. "Meow!"

Stephanie saw that the cat had gone from mellow to tense. Something was afoot.

"He's trying to tell us something," Stephanie said.

Familiar ran to the back door and began to claw frantically at it.

As soon as she opened the door, the cat shot out into the pinkish-gray morning light. Stephanie grabbed a jacket and was right on the heels of the feline.

When she rounded the corner, she saw what had upset Familiar.

A hooded figure stood at the paddock holding a lead rope attached to Black Jack's halter. Both figures were mere silhouettes against the glowing eastern sky, but Stephanie could clearly see the whip the figure held.

He brought it down across the stallion's back, and Black Jack surged out of the paddock. The man tried to hang on to the lead rope, but he was no match for the panicked horse.

Black Jack reared, his front hooves narrowly missing the figure's head. Then the stallion spun and bolted, the rope dangling dangerously behind him as he galloped away.

"Black Jack!" Stephanie started after the stallion, but Johnny's grasp caught her and stopped her.

"He may have a gun," Johnny warned as he manhandled her back into the relative safety of the cabin. Stephanie caught a glimpse of the hooded figure getting to his feet.

"Black Jack is loose!" Stephanie struggled to free herself.

"You can't go out there." Johnny pressed her against the kitchen wall and held her until she stopped fighting.

"I have to find that horse." Stephanie spat the words.

"And we will. Together. But we have to use some precautions, Stephanie. If that's one of Diego's men, he'll have a gun and he'll use it if you force him into a corner. Now if you'll calm down and stay put, I'll handle this."

She wanted to throttle him. All the tender feelings from a moment before fled. In their place were anger and worry for the horse.

"I'll be right back." Johnny went to the closet and brought out one of the rifles. He held it, barrel pointed down. "Stay in the house."

She clamped her teeth together.

"Promise me?"

He wasn't going to budge until she promised. "I'll stay here," she said, lying through her teeth. What was good for the gander was good for the goose—a bit of wisdom her Grandmother Olga had taught her. Grandmother Olga, a Swedish immigrant, had claimed that she had tamed and trained Grandfather Running Horse just as he had gentled the wild horses.

Somewhere along the line, Stephanie had to concede that maybe she should have spent more time with Grandmother Olga, learning those important lessons about men.

"Don't come outside," Johnny said as he opened the back door. He didn't wait for an answer.

JOHNNY SLIPPED OUT the door, hot on the trail of Familiar. He could hear the pounding of Black Jack's hooves growing softer and softer. The stallion had headed west.

While Johnny worried about the horse, he was far more worried about the figure near the paddock. Judging from the size of the frame, it was a man, who ran and straddled an ATV. He tried to kick the vehicle into life but the engine only coughed and failed to catch.

Johnny ran. He was nearly at the four-wheel vehicle when the engine caught. Johnny launched himself into a flying tackle, grasping the rider's shoulders in an attempt to unseat him. But the driver ducked and held on to the handlebars of the machine. Swerving back and forth, he successfully dislodged Johnny.

As Johnny rolled in the dust, the intruder gunned the engine of the ATV and took off. By the time Johnny regained his footing, the trespasser was fifty yards away and traveling too fast to catch.

Cursing, Johnny stood, dusted off his pants and went to the paddock to see if any clues had been left behind.

Familiar had beaten him there, and the black cat was batting something in the tall grass by the paddock gate.

Johnny knelt beside the cat to examine the area. To his surprise, the rising sun glinted on something shiny. He picked up the cuff link. It was heavy gold with a vine twined around an ornate *D*.

Carlos Diego loved to display his wealth. He was known as an elegant dresser who often wore cuff links, gold chains and diamond rings. Even his gunmen wore French cuffs with Diego's signature gold links. The *D* led Johnny to believe that the cuff link belonged to one of Diego's minions. But why would Carlos Diego want a horse, particularly one as dangerous as Black Jack? As leverage, or perhaps an act of terrorism that would bring Stephanie to heel.

He pocketed the cuff link just as he heard Stephanie running up behind him.

"Get the truck," she ordered. "Hurry. I'll grab a bucket of feed. Maybe we can stop him before he gets to the ravine."

Before he could say anything, she was gone, running to find a bucket and some feed. Now wasn't the time for negative thoughts. He was worried about the horse, too. He ran to his truck, cut a sharp U-turn, and stopped as Stephanie and Familiar ran out of the shed. They both climbed into the pickup.

"Who was that man?" Stephanie asked.

Johnny hesitated. When he felt her gaze on him, her anger growing, he explained, "I didn't get a look at him, but I found a cuff link with a *D* engraved on it. He must be one of Diego's men. It's one of Diego's trademarks that his men are well dressed. They all wear French cuffs and cuff links with his signature *D* on them."

She nodded and was silent for a moment as the truck sped down the little-used ranch road. "Why would Diego want a horse?" she finally asked.

"Maybe to bargain with."

"Or maybe to send a message," she said, voicing what he didn't have the heart to tell her. Carlos was the kind of man who would think nothing of killing a horse—or a child—to make his point. He was utterly ruthless.

"But Black Jack got away," he pointed out.

"And is running wild with a lead rope attached to a halter. If it catches on deadfall and he can't break free, he'll die of thirst."

Johnny had thought of everything she said, but he hadn't wanted to mention it. Stephanie was a realist, though. She was horsewoman enough to see the hard facts.

"We'll find him," Johnny said, determined to recover the stallion. "Black Jack is smart. He may end up back at the ranch on his own."

"There's a group of wild horses that winter down in the ravine," she said slowly.

Johnny nodded. "That's likely where he'll head."

Stephanie rubbed between her eyes. "When Black Jack first came here, I considered letting him go, giving him his freedom. He's young and strong and powerful, and I haven't seen the old stallion that ran with the wild herd all summer. I actually thought that maybe the kindest thing I could do for Black Jack was to let him revert to the wild."

Johnny let her talk. Worry had made her taut as a bowstring. Talking might be the only thing that would help her unwind. "Maybe it would be best," he said softly. "I think Black Jack could adapt to a wild life. At least he wouldn't have to go back to Rupert."

She bit her lip. "Believe me, I considered it. But I'm afraid Rupert would shoot the entire herd. He's like that, as you've seen. I don't have a choice. I have to catch Black Jack."

"Then that's what we'll do."

"Me-ow!" Familiar let out a cry and patted his paw against the dash.

"I think he's pointing north," Stephanie said.

Johnny slowed the truck and finally stopped. He got out and began to investigate the ground. The sun was fully up and the light was good, showing a series of footprints in the hard earth. Just as Familiar had thought, the horse had left the ranch track and had headed into the rolling range lands.

It was going to be hell trying to find him, but Johnny was determined to do just that. Find Black Jack and bring him home.

Chapter Eleven

While we have no option but to search for Black Jack, it's occurred to me that this whole horse thing may have been a ruse to get us out of the cabin so someone could search the place. We'll know if that's true when we return.

Maybe I should have raised this issue, but what's the point? Johnny can't leave Stephanie alone at the ranch to defend it. Nor can he allow her to search for Black Jack alone while he guards the cabin. Communicating my concerns will only make a bad situation worse.

For now, Black Jack is the focus. I have to say, though, it makes me a little uncomfortable to be driving along, here on the open range. For right now, there isn't tremendous danger because the land is flat where we are. But ahead, where the hills rise up, men could be hiding. Trust me, I watched enough John Wayne movies to recognize a potential ambush. The Duke would be on red alert, because a sniper could shoot Miss Cowgirl and Johnny from a higher vantage point. We need to find that bronc and get back to the ranch.

If I could reach Eleanor and let her know our situation, she could use her influence in Washington, D.C., to get some help out here. My human daddy, Peter Curry, D.V.M., tends the pampered pets of some of the most powerful people on Capitol Hill. In other words, he has juice. And Eleanor is no slouch. Her university work puts her in contact with those who pass as brainiacs in the biped race. Most are plenty smart in the book sense, but they often lack what I like to call "walking around sense." Still, they have power. They can get things done. If Eleanor and Peter had any idea what was going on at Running Horse Ranch, they'd be on the phone to some senators and law enforcement officials so fast...

The problem is, I'm not certain who's involved in this Omega and who isn't.

Johnny said Omega is a project, not a branch of law enforcement. That tells me it's interdepartmental. And if Carlos Diego is brokering counterintelligence, then the people working in Project Omega must be the James Bonds of the U.S. intelligence community. Rory Sussex must be one whale of a talent. He's managed to play the U.S. government, his friends and Carlos Diego. Man, if he's found alive, I wouldn't want to be in his shoes.

But is Rory alive? This is the elephant in the room no one is talking about. Are Miss Cowgirl and Johnny facing two foes—Diego and a renegade Rory Sussex?

How much more complicated can things get? Eleanor told me that I needed a vacation and how wonderful it would be to relax at Running Horse Ranch. Relax? Right. Not in this lifetime.

Looks like Johnny is slowing the truck. We're closer to the ridge of hills, and I don't like this at all. Okay, I see what it is. A lead rope is lying in the dirt. And on closer inspection, I see that it didn't break. Someone unsnapped it.

Oh, dear. The implications of this go far beyond inter-esting. First of all, who could get close enough to that horse to unsnap the lead? And why?

This doesn't bode well at all.

STEPHANIE PICKED UP THE ROPE and examined it. Her fingers traced the twisted cotton, and Johnny could almost read her thoughts. The lead was in good shape, the snap in working order. She clicked the snap again and again.

Johnny knew the only explanation was that someone had deliberately removed it from Black Jack's halter. But why not remove the halter, too? And how had they gotten hold of the horse long enough to unhook the lead?

He searched the area, looking for the bright red piece of tack. He saw nothing, except for footprints that led to the rope and then away. Back to what appeared to be ATV tire tracks.

He watched as Stephanie read the same story in the dirt. "You think it was the same guy who was at the ranch this morning?" she asked.

Johnny shook his head. "I can't tell. The tread isn't dis-tinctive enough. It's just a rough impression in the sand."

"I know."

Johnny had come to respect her skills. She was enough of a tracker to realize that the prints left by whoever had unhooked Black Jack's lead told no clear story.

"We should get out of here." Johnny scanned the horizon. "We're sitting ducks if someone wants to shoot us."

"I'll bet they're all at the ranch having a field day going through the cabin and the sheds," Stephanie said.

Johnny didn't bother to hide his surprise. "You thought of that, too?"

"It was the first thing that crossed my mind. But what could we do except pursue Black Jack?"

"At least he's not going to get hung somewhere," Johnny pointed out.

"I'd feel better if the halter had been removed, too, but you're right. This greatly improves his chances of survival."

"Shall we keep hunting for him?" Johnny surveyed the area.

"I think we need to go back and get some horses. We'll be able to track him on horseback. He's less likely to be upset by a horse than a vehicle chasing after him."

"That's the worst—" He bit back his response. Stephanie wasn't the kind of woman who took kindly to criticism of what she deemed to be necessary.

"He's fond of Piper and Layla," she said, as if explaining that that would make it less dangerous. "If he hasn't hooked up with the wild herd, maybe he'll come to one of the mares."

It wasn't a bad plan. In fact, had there not been the possibility of a sniper, Johnny would have proposed the exact same plan. But she read his disapproval. He saw it in the way her face fell.

"I'm sorry, Stephanie. I think with the lead rope removed, the worst danger is over. We should let Black Jack take care of himself."

"There are a million reasons he may not be able to do that," she said slowly.

"I know." He couldn't stop himself. He put his hand on her shoulder. It was a gesture of support and comfort, but he was aware of the sexual charge as soon as he touched her. "There's another way of looking at this, though. Black

Jack is probably safer out here. I don't think anyone can catch him. No one can burn the barn down around him or shoot him while he's penned in a corral. He may be better off running free."

Stephanie sighed. "You may be right about that. What about the other horses?"

Johnny considered his answer. "I don't think Diego will let you drive out of here with them loaded in a trailer. Worst case, he could shoot out a tire and wreck the rig." He was frightening her. He could see it, and he didn't like it, but he'd vowed to tell her the truth, at least as much as he could without further endangering her.

"So we're prisoners here?"

"Pretty much. Maybe we should turn the horses out. We'll round them up later, when this is over."

"Tex is injured. If he gets out here, running…"

Johnny hid his worry. She had enough of a burden to carry. "I know, but he's a smart horse. He'll look out for himself. I'm afraid if I don't let him go, he'll end up being target practice for one of Diego's men."

Stephanie threw the lead rope in the back of the pickup. "Then let's go. The more daylight they have, the better their odds at finding a safe place to graze."

Johnny wanted to hold her, to try to offer at least the comfort of his arms. But he didn't. He let her walk back to the truck and climb in the passenger seat, the black cat right at her side like a shadow.

He got behind the wheel and drove back to the ranch, dreading with each mile what he might find when he got there.

STEPHANIE SEARCHED THE HORIZON, terrified that she'd see smoke from another blaze set by Diego and his men. But the sky was pale blue, and when they could see the ranch, all the buildings were intact and the horses milled around in the corrals and paddocks.

"It doesn't look like anyone was here," Stephanie said, wondering if she were seeing only what she wanted to see.

Johnny didn't say anything, which told her he would check and evaluate the whole ranch before he gave an opinion.

He pulled the truck up against the barn where they had the most sheltered exit. "Run for the cabin," he told her. "But be cautious. I don't think anyone's in there, but never take anything for granted."

"Where are you going?" she asked.

"To open the corrals and paddocks."

"I'll help you."

He grasped her arm firmly. "Please, Stephanie. Get inside. Let me do this."

"Okay," she said. Without another word, she slipped out of the truck and darted across the open space to the back door. In a moment she was inside.

Stephanie barely cleared the doorway when she stopped. The cabin felt like enemy terrain. Pressing herself against the kitchen wall, she looked around the room, searching for evidence that someone had been there.

Or might still be there.

Her ears were attuned to the slightest noise, and when the refrigerator motor kicked on, she almost jumped. Covert work wasn't for her. She hated this.

She took two steps into the kitchen and stopped. The sound of the clock ticking was too loud. She couldn't think.

The dishes from breakfast remained in the drainboard, the bowl of apples on the table. She couldn't tell if anyone had been in the room or not.

Had she left the silverware drawer askew? She couldn't remember. She moved into the room, careful to keep her footsteps muffled. If an intruder were in the house, she had to be sure she'd didn't alert him.

She tiptoed to the closet where Johnny had put the guns and grasped one. She didn't like firearms, but she knew how to use them. Rory had taught her. She'd been amused at how proficient he seemed with guns. Now it wasn't amusing at all.

She checked the rifle, making sure it was loaded. A handgun would be easier to maneuver in the cabin, but she'd make do with what she had.

Creeping around the cabin, she surveyed everything. Nothing seemed amiss. She went to her bedroom and stopped. The contents of her jewelry box were scattered across her bed.

For a second she couldn't catch her breath. The evidence that someone had entered her home, had violated her security, was like a punch to her stomach. When she could finally draw in oxygen, she checked the bathroom and closet to be sure no one was hiding.

At last she went to the bed. She wasn't a woman with a lot of jewelry. She had several family pieces that held more sentimental value than monetary worth. She searched for those, relieved to find the two rings there. She reached up and touched the earrings she wore. Those were the only thing Rory had given her. The earrings were whimsical— wires and beads in a colorful pattern.

Nothing was missing.

Whoever had gone through her belongings had not taken a single thing.

So whatever he was looking for he hadn't found.

JOHNNY COLLECTED the remaining weapons in his truck and locked it. Placing most of the guns in the truck bed, he selected a Glock and tucked it into his waistband. Moving out of the protection of the truck, he yielded to his senses.

The ranch was quiet. Too quiet. The horses seemed peaceful enough, but there wasn't a bird or any other small creature moving on the property. The acrid smell of the burned barn still hung in the air, a reminder of how dangerous Carlos Diego could be.

Johnny ran to the first corral. He opened the gate wide, moving on to the paddocks and opening them. Once he got one horse to start running, the others would follow.

When all the gates were open, he led Tex and Layla out.

"Be safe," he whispered to them as he slapped Layla on the rump and sent her running toward the wide-open vista of the range. Tex followed, limping only slightly.

When the other horses realized that they were free to go, they bolted through the open gate, and in a moment the entire herd was on the run, galloping toward freedom and, he hoped, safety.

He was heading toward the bunkhouse when the first gunshots kicked dust not two inches from his feet. He didn't try to determine where the shots were coming from. Instead, he dove headlong onto the bunkhouse porch, rolled, and stumbled through the door as slugs hit the wood beside his shoulder.

Johnny slammed the door shut and drew the pistol at his waist. He'd left the rifles, which would have been far more effective, in the bed of the truck.

Glancing out the window, he didn't see anyone. Judging by the angle of the shots that had struck the porch, the gunman was positioned in the west. Now, in the morning, the sunlight would be in the shooter's eyes.

But the strange thing was that the gunman had had a number of clear shots. He should have been able to take Johnny out at any time. Yet he'd waited.

Was Diego playing with them, terrorizing them in an effort to soften them up for when he made his move? That was a favorite ploy of Diego's, Johnny recalled.

Johnny scanned the bunkhouse. There was no evidence that anyone had been there, searching. Which Johnny found strange. Letting Black Jack loose had obviously been designed to get them off the ranch. And it had worked. He wondered if Stephanie had discovered any signs of a search in the cabin.

Johnny heard shattering glass and looked out to see the windows on his truck explode. Next went the tires. The truck was rendered inoperable.

Stephanie's truck was parked under the toolshed lean-to roof. How long would it be before they took that out—if they hadn't already done something to disable it?

A curtain fluttered in the cabin window, and he saw Stephanie's face pale with worry. He waved her away from the window.

As soon as he could, he'd make it to the cabin. Once there, he and Stephanie would have to come to an agreement about what to do next.

Chapter Twelve

Stephanie stared at her image in the bathroom mirror. The earrings peeked out from beneath her long chestnut hair. Very carefully she reached for one and then the other, removing them, holding them gently as she examined them in the bright fluorescent light.

Brilliantly colored gemstones were interspersed with pieces of colored wire, tiny cogs and what appeared to be computer chips. The juxtaposition of natural stone and manmade technology had first drawn her interest at a street festival in Gulf Shores. She and Rory had been walking along, examining the wares in the booths that had been set up with the rushing aqua surf in the background. They'd laughed and held hands as they checked out pottery, drawings, CDs by local musicians, wood carvings, quilts and other artistic and handcrafted goods.

When she saw the earrings and picked them up, she'd been merely curious, then captivated by the strange beauty of the craftsmanship. Later, Rory had slipped back to the booth and purchased them as a surprise for her.

Now she knew why.

There was not one single aspect or action of Rory

Sussex that hadn't been designed to move his plan forward.

She held the earrings up to the light one by one. She couldn't see the microchip, but she knew it was there. Implanted by Rory and given to her for safekeeping. He'd really trusted her ability to care for things. It would have been easy for her to accidentally lose the earring. But he knew how she took care of things that had sentimental value to her. He'd seen the way she cared for his letters and the photographs of her grandparents.

He'd known her so much better than she'd ever known him. She'd willingly shown him her heart and spirit, trusting that he'd do the same. The only thing he'd shown her, though, was a carefully constructed facade, one that had pulled her into a life of danger. She could never forgive him for that.

The temptation to grind the earrings to dust on the slate bathroom floor was almost overwhelming. She resisted, though. Whatever was encoded on the chip in the earrings must have great value. Perhaps enough to use as a bargaining tool for her and Johnny's lives, should it come down to it.

For the first time, she understood the dilemma Johnny faced. Should she tell him about the earrings? By sharing that knowledge, she was also putting him deeper in danger. And perhaps a lot of other people. Whatever was on the microchip was valuable—to both the forces of good and evil. Lives were undoubtedly at stake.

She hadn't asked for this knowledge, or this decision. But she had to make it. Everything that had happened at the ranch had been visited upon her by forces outside her life. First Rory, now Carlos Diego and his henchmen, and even Johnny had taken control of events, and she'd been forced into a powerless position. The horses in her care had been endangered, and everything she'd worked for was in jeopardy. Once Johnny knew about the microchip, he would be forced to take action, and that might mean even more danger. Now, for this one moment, she held the key and she had a choice. Later, if necessary, she would share what she knew with Johnny. But not until there was no other option.

She was still musing over the earrings when she heard the first shot. Dropping the jewelry into the top drawer in the bathroom cabinet, she hurried to the bedroom window where she had a view of the bunkhouse. She was just in time to see the glass on Johnny's truck shattered by gunfire and his tires deflated by still more bullets. Johnny had been smart to turn the horses out when he had. And he was right—Carlos Diego had no intention of letting her or Johnny leave the ranch.

They were in it for the long haul, and they were going to have to fight for their lives.

She picked up the gun and went to the front of the house. She couldn't tell exactly where the sniper was firing from. There were several small rises that could hide a careful man. She cracked the door open and eased the barrel out.

"You can dish it out. Let's see if you can take it," she said softly through clenched teeth as she sighted on one of the rises and fired six rounds in rapid succession.

Once the echo of the shots died away, the silence was almost deafening.

The door of the bunkhouse opened and Johnny rushed toward the cabin, running and rolling only to come up on his feet still running. He hit the back door with the force of his body and blasted into the ranch house.

"Get away from the door," he ordered, as if she were a moron.

That aggravated her to the point that she swung around to face him. "Don't tell me what to do." She held the rifle carefully pointed at the ground, and she saw that he took note of that fact. "Rory taught me to shoot and to handle a gun. I thought it was a hobby of his. You know in the first blush of love how you're willing to share interests? Well, this was one of his, and I shared it."

She started out the door, but Johnny grabbed her and pulled her back inside.

"Do you want to get killed?" he asked her. He glanced outside.

"I don't want any of this," she answered, her fury escalating at an alarming pace.

Johnny studied the terrain. "I think they're gone now. They're playing with us. When they get serious, we'll know it."

"I'm sick of this." She stomped into the kitchen. Her anger was so overwhelming that she couldn't decide where to aim it. She put the rifle on the kitchen table and went to the cabinets. She pulled out Rory's favorite coffee mug and smashed it onto the floor. The crystal vase he'd brought flowers to her in was next, then the crockery he'd admired.

She pulled dish after dish out of the cabinets and smashed them. She didn't realize that she was crying—not silent tears but great heaving sobs of emotion. And with each crash of a dish, she cried harder.

Johnny stood in the doorway. He made no move to stop

her. He merely watched. He put his pistol on the table beside the rifle and waited for the storm to pass.

Stephanie was halfway through her dishes when she gained control of her emotions. She stopped, a plate held high in one hand. She put the plate down and grabbed a paper towel to wipe her face.

Before she knew what was happening, she felt Johnny's arms around her. He turned her in to his chest and held her, one hand stroking her hair.

This time her tears were quiet, fueled by grief and loss more than anger. Rory had robbed her of something she'd guarded all her life—an innocent belief that people would give their best if they had that opportunity. It was true of horses and dogs—and cats, if Familiar was representative of his species. And she'd believed it of people. She'd been so careful not to allow the wrong kind of folks into her life, those who would use and betray her. But she'd opened her heart to Rory, believing every word he'd said.

"I'm such a fool," she said, pressing into the soft cotton of Johnny's shirt. "How could I be so stupid? How could I have had so many signs and heeded none of them? 'Oh, let's go learn to shoot, Stephanie,'" she mocked herself.

Johnny shushed her, one hand stroking her hair and the other gently rubbing her back. She could feel the warmth through her shirt, and her body responded before her brain could.

The comfort he gave her so naturally was something she needed. Ever since she'd learned of Rory's plane crash and supposed death, she'd been totally alone, completely focused on surviving and hanging on to the dream they'd shared. She hadn't allowed herself a moment of softness, because she'd been afraid she'd break and would never be able to pull herself together again. The horses depended on her to be strong, to carry on the daily routine.

Now, though, even if just for a moment, Johnny was holding her. His hands caressed her, moving lower down her back. He kissed the top of her head, his lips moving down to her cheek. Even if it was weakness—even if it was only for this moment—she needed someone to be strong for her.

Stephanie raised her chin. Her lips met Johnny's. The fire that was suddenly kindled burned away the remnants of her sorrow. In a split second, she stepped out of her grief and into an overwhelming passion.

Her arms circled Johnny's neck and his hands moved down her back, past her waist, pulling her against him with a power that took her breath away.

The kiss seared through her, and she knew he was feeling the same thing. Whatever the reasons for this passion, she didn't want to analyze them. Johnny was holding her, kissing her, making her feel things she'd never felt before, reminding her that her life wasn't over.

His arm swept beneath her legs and he lifted her into his arms. He carried her into the bedroom and put her on the bed. His hands shook slightly as he worked the buttons of her shirt.

In a moment he had her undressed, and he removed his own clothes.

"Are you sure?" he asked.

That one question told her, without a doubt, how sure she was.

"Yes." She met his gaze. She'd used caution with Rory, had insisted on a traditional time to date and get to know each other before the relationship escalated to intimacy. None of that had mattered in the long run. And there was no guarantee, with Carlos Diego waiting outside the cabin, that they'd have another chance. "Yes, I'm positive."

Johnny took the invitation. He was beside her on the bed, slowly exploring her body as she let her hand wander over the long, lean muscles of his thighs and the ridges of his stomach. She noted the scar that ran from below his left nipple to his hip bone. Later, she'd ask about it, even though she probably wouldn't want to hear the story.

Johnny was as dangerous and unpredictable as Black Jack. He'd come into her life on a pretext and falsehood, and he'd likely leave the same way. If they were both alive to part ways.

Whatever the end result, she needed to be loved by Johnny Kreel. She could live with her sorrow for the rest of her life, but for this moment she wanted only the passion that he aroused.

WELL, OKAY, THEN. Miss Cowgirl has kicked over the traces and gone for broke. I wish I could say I'm surprised. The sexual tension between those two has been thick enough to cut with a knife.

Speaking of knife, I wonder if I can get some grub. While the humanoids may be able to live on love alone, this feline needs food.

I'll saunter to the kitchen and check out the refrigerator door. Yep. I can open it. And there are some tasty leftovers within reach. I just need to pull out that container with my paw. Not to worry about making a mess. Miss Cowgirl has already pretty much destroyed the kitchen. What's a bit of salmon on the floor with all the broken dishes?

I like a woman with a temper well enough, but it can get a little costly. Luckily, that's not my concern.

Now that I've had a tasty snack, I'll keep an eye out for invading criminals. While hot sex is great, I want to live to lust another day. Good thing the bipeds have me to watch out for them. I'm sure Johnny knows his business, but there were shots aimed in our direction not so long ago.

The horizon is clear, it's true. Johnny may know how this Diego character works. I suppose I can take a little snooze here in the window. Cats, remarkable creatures that we are, can sleep and stand guard. We are masters at multitasking, as long as one task involves sleeping or eating.

I'll climb up here on the windowsill where the sun has warmed the wood and doze a little bit. No telling when I'll get another chance. I'll dream of being home in Washington with my Clotilde.

When Stephanie and Johnny finish with the business at hand, we need to see if we can get an Internet connection working and do some research. I know the phones have been down. I've seen Johnny trying to call—without success. If we truly are isolated, then we need to come up with an escape plan. The available options sure don't look appealing to a black cat with an aversion to riding horses.

THE AFTERNOON SUN SLANTED through the bedroom window and hit the golden highlights in Stephanie's hair that spread across the pillow. Exhausted and spent, she'd fallen asleep. Now he had a moment to study her without making her uncomfortable.

She was a beautiful woman. One worth any amount of risk. Rory had always been able to draw women to him like flies to honey. And he'd never felt bad that he was selling them a total fabrication of his life. Johnny had never approved, because he'd always suspected that the women paid a heavy price when Rory disappeared. Now he knew how much pain Rory left in his wake.

Stephanie didn't deserve that kind of grief. No one did. Johnny could only hope that somehow she'd be able to see that he was not like Rory. That she'd eventually allow him to love her.

He brushed a strand of hair from her face, marveling at the softness of her skin. She was a remarkable blend of strength and tenderness. Rory Sussex had been a total moron to involve her in a scheme that put her in such danger.

Anger at Rory flared through him, but he tamped it down. For this moment, at least, he had to let it go. He had to focus on getting Stephanie safely away from Carlos Diego.

Stephanie was sleeping so soundly that he suspected she'd had little rest for the last few days. He slipped an arm from beneath her and pulled on his clothes.

He walked through the small cabin, noting Familiar in the window. The cat had kept watch. Johnny felt a moment of chagrin that he'd failed to keep his own defenses on red alert, but the cat would have let him know had anything been amiss. In fact, Familiar was the best partner he'd ever worked with.

At the window he stroked Familiar's back and checked the horizon. All appeared quiet. The horses had, no doubt, gone to find water. Tex worried him. The gelding needed care and attention, and as soon as this Diego mess was resolved, he'd find him and make it up to him.

Sighing, he went to the kitchen, found a broom and dustpan and began the slow process of sweeping up the broken dish shards.

Once that was done, he began a systematic search of the cabin. Somewhere, Rory had hidden something. Something of great value. Not money. Not diamonds. It had to be information, and that made the job of finding it much more difficult, because it could be encoded on the tiniest of chips.

"Meow."

He looked down to find Familiar sitting on his boot.

"What's up?" he asked the cat.

Familiar sauntered over to the computer and tapped the keyboard.

"Very clever," he said. He doubted that Rory would put the information on Stephanie's hard drive, but it was worth a check. He wasn't a hacker, but he had some basic knowledge.

He sat down and turned on the machine. Familiar nudged the mouse with his nose until it centered over the Internet browser.

"Want to go online?" he asked Familiar.

"Meow."

Johnny tried several times, with no luck. "Let me check something." He debated going outside, but there was only one way to check. He slipped out the back door. It only took a few seconds for him to discover that the wire to the satellite dish had been severed and several feet of it were missing.

"Dammit," he said. He hurried back to the cabin. "We're totally cut off," he told the cat.

Familiar hopped back into the window, his attention focused on the three small rises where the sniper had been hiding.

The cat's behavior didn't make Johnny feel any more at ease. Familiar expected an attack, which confirmed Johnny's gut feeling. As soon as night came, Diego would make his move.

Johnny returned to the kitchen and reloaded the rifle Stephanie had shot. He checked the rifle with the nightscope, and he double-checked his own weapon. Somehow, he needed to get to the truck and retrieve the weapons he'd stashed there. They'd need all the firepower they could get.

He hated to leave Stephanie alone while she was asleep, but it might be best if he went now. He was about to step out the back door when the cat blocked his path.

"I'll be right back," he said. He tried to step around Familiar, but the feline blocked him again. There was something in the cat's green gaze that stopped him. Familiar was not to be trifled with. The cat was smart.

Slowly he closed the door. "Okay," he said, "I'll take your warning."

Familiar rubbed against his shins, purring.

Until Stephanie awoke, he'd continue to search the cabin. If he could just find what Rory and Diego were after, he might have enough bargaining power to get the three of them off the ranch alive.

Chapter Thirteen

Stephanie knew she was dreaming. At first, she'd found herself standing in the sunshine, the vista of the Black Hills ahead of her. In the distance was her grandfather, Running Horse. He rode toward her on Black Jack, and even from so far away she knew that he was smiling at the good work she'd done on the stallion. The horse was perfectly attuned to every shift of his weight, as responsive as if they shared each other's most intimate thoughts.

The closer they drew to her, the happier Stephanie felt. It was a perfect South Dakota day. The blue sky was filled with warmth, but not nearly as warm as the pride she saw in her grandfather's eyes when he rode up to her.

"You've carried on my teachings," he said, his brown, leathered face slowly pulling into a rare smile. "The secrets of my blood have passed to you."

"I hope so, Grandfather," she answered.

Running Horse nodded to the west. "There's a storm coming," he said. "Take cover and beware of snakes."

When she looked beyond him, she saw the black clouds gathering. A moment before they hadn't been there.

"Be careful," he said. "I have to go."

"Stay with me." Stephanie had rarely asked for anything except the opportunity to learn from him. "Please, Grandfather. I don't want to be here alone."

He nodded. "But you aren't alone."

He wheeled Black Jack and rode to the north, to the hills where the Sioux people originated.

Stephanie thrashed in her sleep. The emotions evoked by the dream were so strong that they almost awakened her. She was aware that the bed was empty, that Johnny had left her, too. A part of her was alarmed, urging her to wake up. But the physical and emotional exhaustion of the past several days pulled her back under. She yielded to sleep and found herself in another dream state.

This time she was in her bedroom. The room was totally dark. Night had fallen. The darkness was electric with danger, and she was trapped and tangled in the sheets.

There was the creak of a window opening. When she glanced in the dresser mirror, she could see the sash slowly inching up. She could see the black-gloved hand that slipped out of the night and gripped the bottom of the panes. Very slowly the window opened wider and wider.

Watching in fascinated horror, she saw the foot and leg come through into the bedroom.

Everything happened in slow motion, and she couldn't rouse herself to do a thing.

"Help!" She thought she called out, but she couldn't be sure. The line between dream and reality had blurred.

"Help me!" she tried again.

There was the sound of something pounding against the bedroom door, then footsteps running down the hallway.

The figure in the window withdrew.

The bedroom door burst open and Familiar was across

the room like a flash of black lightning. He leaped through the open window and into the darkness.

There was a startled human yelp and the yowl of a furious feline, a sound as primitive as that of a hunting puma.

Johnny was right behind the cat, bursting into the room and grasping her arms as he leaned over the bed.

"Stephanie, are you hurt?" he asked.

"Someone was breaking in." It wasn't a dream. That was the terrible part of it. The window was open and cold air flooded the room. She shivered and dragged the covers up.

Not bothering to go back through the house and out the door, Johnny drew his gun and dove through the window.

Stephanie struggled out of the bed, feeling as if she'd been drugged. When the blast of cold air from the window struck her, the last vestiges of sleep fled. She was fully awake and terrified.

Outside she heard running, but she couldn't see anything. Remembering the rifle with the nightscope, she rushed to the kitchen and grabbed it. Barefoot and un-clothed, she went to the window and set up for a shot at the intruder—if she got the opportunity.

It was hard to adjust to the vision the scope allowed, a single circle of vague imagery. But she identified Johnny and Familiar and, farther in the distance, a man in black, fleeing.

The intruder was a hundred yards away when he climbed on a four-wheeler. The machine roared to life.

Stephanie had a clear shot. She'd never considered that she might point and fire a weapon at another human being, but she didn't hesitate. She made sure Johnny and Familiar were not in her way, took aim and squeezed the trigger.

The man on the four-wheeler cut the wheel, almost

wrecking. But he kept going until he was out of sight and the sound of the ATV disappeared.

She lowered the rifle and waited for Johnny and Familiar to return. Her heart was pounding and she felt sick to her stomach. She'd wounded the man. There was no doubt about it.

The thing that made her sick was how glad she was that she'd done it.

JOHNNY FOUND FAMILIAR hovering over the blood spot on the ground. He'd been surprised that Stephanie had shot at the intruder, but he shouldn't have been. She was fighting for the things she loved. While she might not kill to save herself, she would to save a human life or the horses.

Using a small laser penlight, he examined the blood. It wasn't a huge amount. She'd likely winged the intruder. At least Carlos Diego would know they weren't going down without a fight.

"We'll check this out properly tomorrow," he told the cat. He was a little worried about his absence from Stephanie. It seemed as if every time he turned his back on her, something happened.

They went inside, and Johnny found Stephanie standing at the kitchen sink, trembling.

"Sit down, Stephanie," he said gently. He helped her into a chair. She was white as a sheet and suffering from shock. He placed a shot of whiskey in front of her and waited for her to take a sip.

"You were only protecting yourself," he said.

"What kind of life is this that I have to shoot someone to protect myself?" She sipped the whiskey slowly.

"The kind that you didn't choose. This will be over soon, Stephanie. I swear it."

"He was almost in the window."

Johnny didn't need that pointed out to him. He was already kicking himself for his carelessness. He'd expected an attack from Diego, but not a B&E attempt. It was more Diego's style to surround the cabin with henchmen armed with automatic weapons and keep them blasting until nothing was left. Diego was not a man given to subtle gestures.

In fact, the whole thing didn't smell right. By all rights, Diego should have made his move by now, and he should have wiped the ranch off the map. The gangster had destroyed their ability to communicate with the outside, but Diego was no fool. He had to know that eventually, some federal law enforcement official would show up to check on Johnny. The organization was loosely structured, but there were checks and balances on agents to give them at least a modicum of safety.

Diego had limited time to make his move and recover the information. So what was stopping him? Why would he waste energy on an attempted B&E when he had the firepower to take what he wanted?

"Who did I shoot?"

Stephanie's point-blank question crystallized all his concerns and thoughts. Though he had an idea who it was, his answer was going to be one more lie stacked on top of the others that she would likely never forgive him for. But this was one matter where the only thing he could do was lie, to protect her.

"I don't know. Tomorrow I'll check the blood. I don't think it was a mortal wound."

"Not from lack of trying," she said and swallowed the rest of the whiskey.

He poured her another shot and one for himself.

"I'll go out there at first light," Johnny told her. "I'll find out what I can by the evidence there."

"Why don't they just kill us?" she asked, and there was a steeliness in her tone that made him realize how much the latest turn of events had cost her.

"I don't know," he answered. That much was truthful.

She got up and went to the window. He was relieved to see that she was no longer shaking. Maybe more disturbing was the set of her jaw and the square of her shoulders. She was ready for the long haul, and she would fight every step of the way.

Johnny felt total admiration for her, and guilt for being involved in a situation that pushed her to this point. He knew from personal experience that once a man, or woman, decided that survival was the top priority, it changed him or her. It was a brutal awakening, one he would have gladly spared Stephanie.

"We have to get off the ranch," Stephanie said. She spoke as she gazed out into the black night.

"I don't think we can."

"I'm thinking we're about due from a visit from Rupert Casper. He'll be up here checking on Black Jack. Maybe we can slip into his truck and get away."

It wasn't a bad plan. Johnny had to give her credit for that. "Maybe," he said. His hope rose. "You think he'll come?"

"He can't raise me on the phone and he's surely not going to let it go without checking on Black Jack and making sure I'm not slacking off on the horse. He's been out of town, but he's probably back by now. He'll show up here."

She was probably right about that. Rupert was that kind of guy. "I can't believe I'd ever be glad to see Rupert Casper."

She turned and gave him a wry grin. "Ditto."

"Espionage and survival do indeed make strange bed-fellows."

"I don't think that's the original quote, but it works in this instance." She came back to the table and sat down. "I'm sick over shooting someone."

Johnny knew she would be even sicker if the victim were who he thought it might be. "You were protecting yourself and me and Familiar. You didn't have a choice."

"Oh, we always have a choice."

"Not true. We don't even know what Diego is looking for, what's so important."

"If we knew, would it make a difference?"

"Maybe a big one. Even a hint would be good."

"I don't see how it would change anything."

She sounded so terribly sad. He put his hand on hers and squeezed.

She didn't look at him and slowly withdrew her hand. "Want some coffee?" she asked.

He nodded. "That would be good. We have a few hours until dawn, but I'm not going to sleep."

"Neither am I." She got up and prepared the coffeepot.

Johnny knows something and he isn't sharing it with me or Miss Cowgirl. That's the thing about Feds. They think they've got to control everything. How can we help him— or even protect ourselves—if he continues to withhold information?

And watching that last little exchange between her and Johnny, I'd say Miss Cowgirl has some secrets of her own.

It's like they're both playing on the same team but with different game plans.

So that leaves it to me to find the "valuable" thing that Carlos Diego would want.

Once I figure out what that is, maybe I can hatch a way to get us out of this alive. If it's government secrets or a list of U.S. operatives, we have to destroy it. I don't want to go out in a blaze of glory in South Dakota, but we can't let that kind of list get into the hands of the bad guys. It could jeopardize U.S. agents' safety around the globe.

So I'll start a subtle search.

Uh-oh. What's that thud at the front door? It didn't sound good.

Johnny is running there, pushing Stephanie behind him. He's cracking the door open, and struggling with something stuck in the door.

Oh, good grief. It's an arrow. What! Now we're into some Robin Hood scenario? This guy Diego must be off his rocker. This is a game to him.

Wait, there's something attached to the arrow. It's a...picture.

Judging from the look on Johnny's face, this is not good at all. I hope it isn't Black Jack or one of the other horses. If someone has harmed one of them and taken a photograph, Miss Cowgirl will seek them out and stake them in ant beds.

Johnny is trying to keep the picture from Stephanie, but she's demanding to see it.

He's handing it to her.

Catch her! Great. She went down like she'd been whacked with a hammer. Let me take a look at that picture.

Oh, my, goodness. It's a wounded man, tied and gagged.

And he bears an uncanny resemblance to the long-missing Rory Sussex.

The scales have fallen from my eyes! No wonder Johnny has been evasive. He's suspected all along that Rory was in the area and bedeviling us.

But now he's fallen into the hands of Carlos Diego, who is undoubtedly highly agitato, to quote my friend Kinky Friedman, about being double-crossed. And it would seem that the wound in Rory's shoulder most likely came from the bullet Miss Cowgirl shot.

Oh, guilt and remorse—and a good measure of anger! This is a mess.

To top it off, there's a note on the back of the photo. Johnny has revived Stephanie, and they're reading the note together. It can't be good, judging from the expressions on their faces. If I had to guess, I would say that now Rory is a hostage and will be used in an attempt to force Johnny and Stephanie to give up whatever Diego wants.

The tables have certainly turned.

This time I'm going to have to come up with a brilliant plan to save the day. I need a bit of brain food to get the old noggin going. Let me rummage around the kitchen and see what I can find.

Chapter Fourteen

Stephanie picked up the photograph and stared at the image of Rory Sussex, wounded and in pain, tied and gagged. This couldn't be true. It couldn't be real. Rory's handsome visage was twisted in suffering, and he was looking directly into the camera, as if he knew she'd see the photo and what it would do to her.

Rory was going to die. The horror of it was so big, so overwhelming, that she simply shut down all emotions.

A gun was pointed at Rory's head. The hand holding the gun—a large hand—had a finger depressing the trigger slightly. A twitch and the gun would go off.

Rory was lying on the ground, a sparse grass patch that could be the terrain north of the ranch. Blood had soaked an entire side of his shirt, and he looked tired and dirty.

Nothing else was visible in the photo, which must have been taken within the last few hours, judging from the date and time stamp. Stephanie clung to the numbness, but she knew it wouldn't last. No matter how hard she tried to hold on to it.

"What are we going to do?" she asked Johnny, because she didn't have a clue what their next step should be.

"Rory got himself into this mess. One thing Carlos Diego won't tolerate is a spy." His frustration was clear in his voice and expression. "We don't even know what Diego is after," Johnny pointed out.

His words were like a dagger in her heart. She knew exactly what Carlos Diego wanted. And she knew where to find it, too. All she had to do was say so and then let Johnny do the job he'd been trained for. Let him take responsibility for whatever came down. Hadn't she done enough? She'd shot her fiancé. Technically, her *dead ex*-fiancé, but nonetheless, he had a hole in his shoulder that she'd put there. Had she been a few inches lower or to the right, she would have killed him.

The thought was stunning.

Even if she hadn't killed him, she'd wounded him so that he'd fallen into the hands of a ruthless killer, who would torture or kill him with no compunction.

"How long does Rory have?" she asked. There was always a limit to life in a predicament like this.

"By what I can tell, the wound isn't life-threatening," Johnny answered carefully.

"How long before Diego kills him if we don't respond?"

Johnny paced the room. "Not long. Diego isn't a patient man. But you have to understand, Stephanie, Carlos Diego isn't going to let Rory live no matter what we do."

"We have to try." She tossed the photo onto the table, braced her elbows on her knees and leaned her face into her hands. "They wouldn't have caught him if I hadn't shot him. He would have gotten away."

"Eventually, Diego would have captured him. Besides, that's not even a point worth arguing. Rory betrayed you and he betrayed his country. I don't think he's our first priority."

Stephanie slowly lifted her face. Johnny was angry… and hurt. This was a man she'd made love with only a few hours before. She'd let him into her bed—and her heart. What he couldn't share, though, was her past. No matter what Rory had done, he'd once been someone she cherished. "I understand your point of view, Johnny. But Rory has to be my priority."

She could see the hurt on Johnny's face. She'd cut him deeply. But she couldn't help it.

"Are you still in love with him?" Johnny asked.

She hadn't even considered that possibility. What did she feel for Rory, other than an anger so bright and pure she thought she might actually go up in flames? But there was something there. Some vestige of emotion she couldn't put her finger on or name. "I don't think so. I'm confused."

"But there is a possibility?" Johnny didn't hide the anger in his own tone.

She rose to her feet in indignation. "My fiancé, the man I'd given my heart and future to, crashed his plane in a jungle. His body was never found, but I was told he was dead. I hadn't adjusted to that bit of false information when I discovered that Rory Sussex was a figment of my imagination and the cowhand I hired is also not who he pretends to be."

The longer she talked, the louder she got. "No, both my dead fiancé and the cowhand are spies, secret agents, figures out of some *muy macho* film. And then I shoot my dead ex-fiancé and he falls into the hands of a drug lord who also sells international information. Now he's going to be tortured and killed. And I'm supposed to know how I feel about *any* of this?"

She whirled and stormed out of the room. At the doorway to the hall, she stopped. "I hate Rory and I hate you! I hate this situation and everything about it. The animals in my care are at risk because of you and Rory."

She slammed the door to her bedroom as hard as she could.

JOHNNY FLIPPED THE PHOTO of Rory over. His interest was in the note on the back. "Give me what I want or Sussex will die slowly and painfully."

As Johnny had thought before, Diego was direct and didn't bother with subtlety. He'd kill Rory, and he'd do it in the most painful way, unless he got what he wanted. Then he'd kill him anyway, but maybe at least it would be a swift death.

Even if Johnny had been willing to barter for Rory's life, he didn't have what Carlos Diego wanted. He didn't even know, for sure, what that might be.

He noticed Familiar snooping around the cabin. It was good that at least one member of the team was still on the job. Hell, the cat was the most effective agent he'd ever seen. Familiar had alerted him to the fact that Stephanie was in danger. He'd sensed the intruder and body-slammed the door until Johnny had gotten it open.

Yes, Familiar was keenly alert and sensitive.

He followed the cat into the bathroom and watched as the feline opened the bathroom cabinet and used his paw to move the scant items around. There was little in the cabinet besides dental supplies and a bottle of aspirin.

Satisfied, Familiar shut the cabinet door.

He moved on to the under-sink compartment and finally returned to the drawers. He had a bit of difficulty getting them open, so Johnny helped him.

When the cat spotted the earrings in the top drawer of the bathroom cabinet, he nudged them with his paw.

"Meow." He looked right at Johnny.

"Stephanie was wearing those yesterday," Johnny recalled. They were striking pieces of jewelry. He normally didn't notice earrings like those, but they were highly unusual. He picked them up.

Familiar, claws carefully sheathed, took a swipe at them.

Johnny studied them more closely. He'd never seen anything quite like them, and they'd certainly caught the cat's interest. Was it possible…

"Me-ow!" Familiar's opinion was clear.

He carefully put the earrings back in the drawer until he could find something secure to put them in. He couldn't risk damaging the microchip. Now that he'd found what Rory had hidden at Running Horse Ranch, he had to get it safely out. He stroked the cat's back.

"You are something else, Familiar," he whispered softly. "Come on, buddy, we've got work to do. We need to figure out a way to get to a neighboring ranch or somewhere with phone reception." This situation was bigger than he could manage. He had to get word to Project Omega, and he had to do it fast.

LISTENING AT THE BEDROOM DOOR, Stephanie held her breath while Johnny and Familiar searched the bathroom. If they found the earrings and realized what they were… That couldn't happen. She heard the medicine cabinet close, and then the drawers opening. She couldn't breathe. At last she heard Johnny's footsteps as he left the bathroom.

Once they were gone, she exhaled. It was clear to her what she had to do. The problem was how.

Most of her life she'd believed in right and wrong—a clear distinction between the two. Now she found herself in a world of gray. Not a single course of action open to her was right. Whichever way she chose would have terrible repercussions. Whatever she'd once felt for Rory, that tenderness was gone, but she couldn't let Carlos Diego kill him, either.

The issue was figuring out a way to save Rory without endangering other people—agents spread heaven knew where doing all kinds of jobs, some of them vital to her country.

Her stomach churned at the thought. But the immediate problem was Rory. He'd been captured because she'd shot him. She couldn't go the rest of her life with that on her conscience.

When she was certain Familiar and Johnny were clear of the bathroom, she slipped down the hall and retrieved the earrings. Slipping them into her ears, she couldn't stop the way her hands shook.

Moving through the kitchen, she grabbed her warmest jacket, gloves and a hat. She'd have to walk, and it was cold outside. While she was vaguely worried about finding Diego, she expected he would find her. All she had to do was get away from the ranch and far enough into the open that he spotted her.

She picked up Johnny's gun and tucked it into the waistband of her pants. There wasn't time to find additional ammunition. She also took the rifle with the nightscope. Not that she expected to use it again. Far from it. She had no desire to shoot anyone. But the scope might come in handy.

The back door opened silently and she moved into the still, cold night. In the distance a coyote howled, a sound that had never before seemed sinister. Tonight, though, it seemed like an omen.

She didn't dare look back at the lighted cabin, the safety there. Johnny and Familiar. Despite the circumstances, she'd come to care for Johnny. Deeply. In the crazy reality that had become her life, he was the force for good, the person who was trying to protect her and make this come out right.

But this was something she had to handle on her own.

JOHNNY AND FAMILIAR GAZED OUT the front windows of the cabin. Johnny searched the horizon, counting the minutes until first light. Time was slipping away from him. He felt like a caged animal, trapped within the four walls. He had to go, but he didn't want to leave Stephanie alone. Familiar could stay with her while he tried to use the cover of darkness to trek to Rupert Casper's ranch. It was a long hike, but he was fit. He'd cover the ground as swiftly as possible.

He went to the desk and found paper and a pen. He'd leave Stephanie a note. She'd be furious, but she'd get over it—if any of them survived.

Familiar stood on his back legs and patted Johnny's hand.

"Meow." The cat trotted down the hall and waited at the bathroom door.

"In a minute," Johnny said softly. He was tempted to knock on the bedroom door and try to talk to Stephanie, but another part of him argued that it was best to leave her alone. He hoped she'd fallen asleep.

"Meow!" Familiar was adamant.

Johnny walked down the hallway and watched as Familiar patted the drawers in the bathroom. The cat was certainly determined. Dread settled over Johnny as he opened the top drawer.

"Meow!" Black paws flashing, the cat rummaged through hair clips and cosmetics. "Meow!"

The earrings were gone. Johnny didn't believe it at first, but the sensation that something terrible had moved a step closer to them couldn't be denied. He helped the cat sort through the contents of the drawer. In his head he had a vivid image of the earrings, and awareness came in a flash.

"Stephanie!" He whirled out of the bathroom and ran down the hall. When he knocked on the bedroom door there was no answer.

"Stephanie!" He thrust the door open. The room was empty. "No!" He ran into the kitchen, noting immediately that his Glock was no longer on the table and the rifle was also gone.

Blood thudding in his ears, he understood what had happened. Stephanie had gone out to try to bargain for Rory's life. No doubt, she would lose her own. Diego didn't make deals with anyone, least of all a woman with no power or protection.

He opened the back door and looked out into the night. It was as if the darkness had swallowed Stephanie up. The only sound was a coyote howling in the distance.

She was gone.

Oh, good grief, Miss Cowgirl has lost her mind and set out to find the enemy camp, along with the only thing we could use to bargain—those damn earrings.

From a sane, sensible horse trainer, Stephanie has turned into a rogue operative, except she doesn't fully grasp the ruthlessness of the men she intends to parlay with. This could have a very bad ending. Very bad indeed.

Johnny is frantic. It's plain to see he's fallen head over heels for Stephanie, and I think she cares for him. But this is an honor thing for her. I should have seen it coming. We both should have seen it.

Stephanie couldn't sit back and let Diego kill Rory. She's taken the blame for his predicament, even though it isn't her fault.

So what to do now? We have to track her and find her before she makes it to Diego.

This is where I come in. While I would never, ever compare myself to the lower life-form of the canine, I do have the ability to track by scent. Most cats would never admit this—we don't want to share any traits with a dog. And dogs have allowed this talent to be used against them. They actually work as tracking machines. Gainful employment is not on any kitty's agenda.

But Johnny can't use a light to track Stephanie, so we're going to have to rely on my snozola. And we'd better get out the door and on her trail fast. Perhaps we can overtake her.

Johnny's got the same idea, except he isn't yet aware of how valuable I'm going to be. He's got his coat and his guns. And me.

Hang on, Miss Cowgirl. The cavalry is on the way.

Chapter Fifteen

The night was colder than Stephanie had anticipated. Though it was only October, winter had suddenly arrived. How were the horses getting along? She focused on that worry as she trudged to the north. Flicker would adapt. She was a horse that could survive the hardships of the open range. But what about Tex? He was injured. And Black Jack—had the stallion ever had a moment of real freedom in his entire life? If he'd found the wild herd, he might have challenged one of the other male horses. In doing so, he could have been injured.

The thought made her physically ill, but it was better than thinking about what would happen once Carlos Diego found her. He might kill her to make a point with Johnny. The alternative could be worse.

Try as she might, she couldn't get Rory's anguished face out of her mind. And right beside it was Johnny, the look of betrayal he'd worn when he realized she felt obligated to help Rory. Maybe he was right. Maybe she was a fool to care what happened to a man who'd fed her a plateful of lies. Had she not wounded him… No point going down that road, because she had.

She made it to one of the fence boundaries and slipped

through the wire. Now she was on the range. She allowed herself one glance back at the cabin, a tiny oasis of light on the black horizon.

Was she saying goodbye to the life she'd hoped to build? Maybe. But there wasn't anything she could do to change things. Her hand, warm inside the thick gloves, reached up and tugged at the earrings that dangled from her lobes.

Turning away from the lights of the ranch, she faced north again and began to walk. Far in the distance she heard something. She paused, listening intently. It was the sound of hooves striking the ground. Some of the horses were nearby. She felt a desperate longing to see them, but they were safer away from her.

She continued walking, but she felt the pounding of the hooves grow stronger. The ground vibrated. As she topped a rise, she used the nightscope on the rifle to search for the horses. When they finally came into view, her heart almost stopped.

Black Jack ran at the head of the herd. He was stretched out and magnificent—a true leader. Behind him were Flicker, Piper, Cimarron, Mirage and Layla. Moon Stinger and Dolly's Rocker raced slightly to the west of the other horses. But Black Jack was the leader. He'd created his own herd. Bringing up the rear was Tex, and from the best Stephanie could tell, the gelding was covering the ground without too much difficulty, and Black Jack wasn't giving him any trouble about hanging out with the herd. Sometimes a stallion wouldn't tolerate another grown male horse, not even a gelding.

As if the stallion sensed her watching, he slid to a stop and turned to face her, his mane flowing about his face. Just like a storybook horse, he rose on his hind legs and pawed the air. Before he'd even settled back to the ground, he took off, the other horses following.

She could lay her worries about the horses to rest—for the moment. The sight had restored her faith, though. And her need to fight for the things she loved.

Carlos Diego might be a cruel and clever man, but she had a few tricks up her sleeve as well. Her grandfather was descended from a long line of warriors. The Oglala Sioux were legendary for their caginess, slyness and courage. While she'd never considered herself a warrior, Stephanie was a descendant of people who'd shown true bravery. She could do nothing less now.

And once Rory was saved, she'd kill him herself.

Suddenly, she was blinded by lights pointing directly into her eyes. She threw up her hands to block the glare. Out of the darkness a body hurtled into hers, knocking her to the ground so hard she felt the wind rush out of her lungs. Gasping for breath, she tried to get up, but someone pushed her back down. A big hand on her chest pressed her into the dirt.

"Don't move," a male voice with a foreign accent said.

"I want to talk to Carlos Diego," she managed to wheeze out.

His answer was a laugh that made goose bumps dance over her skin. "You wish to speak to Carlos Diego?" the man mocked her.

"I do." She tried to sit up again, but he pushed her down so hard she couldn't muffle the cry of pain.

"That's funny, because I think Carlos wishes to speak to you." He leaned down so that his foul breath was warm against her cheek. "And once he's done talking, maybe he'll give you to me."

In that instant Stephanie knew that she'd made a terrible mistake. In leaving the ranch, she'd put herself in a position where she had no idea how to protect herself or help Rory. She'd planned to talk to Diego, to use her intellectual wiles to manipulate him. She'd refused to listen to Johnny's warnings or even take into account the lethal threat posed by Diego.

All she'd done by trying to save Rory was put Johnny in danger, because she had no doubt that he'd try to rescue her, even at the risk of his own life.

JOHNNY LAY ON HIS STOMACH on top of a ridge, Familiar at his side. Using the nightscope on his rifle, he'd finally gotten a bead on Stephanie as she trudged through the night. She was a good half mile ahead of him and moving fast. He considered firing a shot into the night to alert her, hoping she'd wait for him to catch up. But something told him not to do that.

When a pair of headlights flared into life, silhouetting Stephanie, he was glad he hadn't given away his position. He watched in fury and concern as the tall figure of a man he recognized as Plenty tackled Stephanie and held her to the ground.

"Dammit, Familiar, they got her," he whispered to the cat.

Familiar was watching intently, and with far better night vision than he had. If the cat could talk, he'd probably be able to relay lots of detail.

Johnny was helpless as he watched Plenty haul Stephanie to her feet and push her toward the vehicle. In a moment she disappeared into the passenger side of an SUV. The vehicle spun in a circle and took off to the north.

Johnny rose to his feet, his hands clenched around the

rifle and a semiautomatic pistol he'd gotten from his truck, along with a pair of night binoculars. There was nothing he could do. Stephanie was taken, and her life hung by the thinnest thread—the whim of Carlos Diego and what he decided to do with her.

"Meow." Familiar sounded as defeated as Johnny felt. There was no way Johnny could catch up with a motorized vehicle. His only recourse was to walk back to the ranch and hope that he could get either his or Stephanie's truck running. That or head to Rupert Casper's place.

"Meow." Familiar put his paws on Johnny's leg. "Meow." The cat nodded.

"You vote that we head to Casper's?"

"Meow." Familiar's head moved up and down.

"That's as good as any plan I can come up with." He hefted the weapons. "Casper's is close, and he'll probably have a working phone or at least a working vehicle. Let's blaze a trail, my friend. If we don't make it fast, Stephanie won't live to see sunrise."

Johnny took his bearings from the stars. He had plenty of wilderness training, and he was in top physical condition. Navigating by the moon and stars, he set out at a ground-covering jog. Familiar was right at his side.

OH, JOY, WHAT THE MILITARY likes to call a forced march. Once we rescue Miss Cowgirl, get Carlos Diego behind bars and see that Rory Sussex is alive to receive punishment for his sins, I'm going to lock myself in Eleanor's library in Washington with Clotilde and we're not going to let anyone in unless they're carrying a tray of delicacies.

Jogging through the frigid October night at the base of the Black Hills is not my idea of fun. I'm more the wine-

and-cheese-party kind of sleuth. Maybe a locked-room mystery in a manor in England. Or, dare I say it, a cruise ship. There's always plenty of food on a ship, and the boats are so big it isn't like really being surrounded by water. And not too much exercise, either. Shuffleboard, drinking, eating, lounging in deck chairs, eating, reading—that sounds spectacular compared to what I'm doing now, which is running like a fool beside Johnny Kreel, cowboy-slash-secret agent man.

Of course all of this whining is to try to keep my mind off what might be happening to Miss Cowgirl. That guy who caught her was pretty rough. He slammed her to the ground like a sack of potatoes. And I got the distinct impression that was only the beginning of what he meant to do to her.

What possessed her to run off and leave Johnny and me? She had to know she was walking into danger. But she did it anyway. And my guess is she's wearing those earrings and she knows they contain the microchip. If that's the case, we don't have a thing to bargain with to save her life.

I don't know what to do, but I can only hope that Johnny can raise some help from the other Omega team members. Right now we have to focus on getting to Rupert Casper's ranch as fast as possible. After that... Well, we'll jump those hurdles when we get to them.

I wonder if Casper might have some sustenance for a cat. Doubtful, and even if his larder were filled with cans of Kitty Delight, he wouldn't share them with me. Even if I starve to death, it will be worth it. Casper deserves much more than I gave him.

But maybe, while Johnny is talking to him, I'll explore his truck again. If his window is down, I'll leave him a reminder of Familiar, Black Cat Detective.

THE SUV HIT SEVERAL BUMPS, hard, and Stephanie felt as if she'd bounce her head on the liner. The man who drove didn't bother glancing at her, but he kept his gun pointed at her. One rash move and he wouldn't hesitate to shoot her, and she knew it. He made it clear that she was beneath contempt. He'd captured her with no effort, and he certainly had no concern that she was a danger.

He'd quickly taken the rifle and the Glock from her. Now she was unarmed—or so he thought. A passenger in a vehicle with a man she recognized as a professional killer.

"What are you going to do with me?" she asked.

He laughed. "When Carlos is done with you, anything I like."

She swallowed her fear. "You can't hurt me, because I have something your boss wants."

"Oh, really?" he said. "What might that be?"

"I'll negotiate only with Carlos Diego."

He laughed again and cut the wheel sharply, causing her to bang her head on the passenger window. Stephanie stifled a cry and resolved to keep silent. This wasn't a man she could convince of anything.

Chances were that Diego would be no easier to trick. She'd come to a poker game with a pair of twos. The only thing left to do was to bluff. So that's what she'd do.

The man flicked his headlights, and in the distance another pair of headlights came on. Fear gripped her. They were driving into the enemy camp.

JOHNNY KEPT UP A STEADY JOG. He'd covered a mile or more, and Rupert Casper's ranch had to be close—if his navigation was correct. Familiar was beside him, running with the same determination and intensity. By cutting cross-country, he'd shaved off at least a mile, but as the minutes ticked by, he knew the danger for Stephanie was increasing exponentially.

Far in the distance he thought he saw the glimmer of lights. Casper's ranch. It had to be. The sight gave him a second wind and new strength in his legs.

The rough terrain made it hard to go faster, but he notched up his speed. The cold air burned in his lungs, but he pushed on. If he could make contact with the head of Omega, Hance Bevins could send in air support. And more men. Whatever it took to save Stephanie and retrieve the information, which he now realized had been a microchip embedded in her earrings. Familiar had pointed that out to him.

As he topped a small rise, he saw the lights of the Casper ranch. It wasn't an illusion. The ranch was within sight. He turned on all the speed he had.

THE SUV CAME TO A SLIDING HALT beside two other vehicles. Stephanie didn't have a chance to do anything before her door was pulled open and she was dragged out and onto the ground. She didn't cry out or make a sound. Begging for mercy wouldn't do any good. She accepted that. And the last thing she wanted was for them to search her.

The man who'd captured her came around the vehicle, leaned down and pulled her to her feet. He pushed her roughly ahead of him, almost causing her to fall as she tripped on the unstable terrain.

"I have a present for you, Carlos," the man said. He pushed her forward again.

She regained her balance and stepped ahead of the man, determined to walk without being pushed. Headlights snapped on, blinding her for a moment. When her eyes adjusted to the light, she saw a figure lying on the ground not twenty feet ahead of her. It took a moment for her to recognize Rory.

He lay bound and unmoving. A tall, slender man dressed in a tailor-made suit stood over him.

"Come to claim your fiancé?" the tall man said, his voice cultured and melodic with a Spanish accent.

"Rory?" She walked toward the body on the ground, afraid that he was already dead. "Rory?"

He moaned and tried to move, but his legs and hands were bound.

"Did you know that your fiancé was a double-crossing traitor?" the tall man asked.

"I don't know anything," Stephanie answered. "I don't know why any of this is happening." The earrings brushed against her cheek in a gust of wind and she was afraid for a moment that her expression would give her away.

"That's too bad," the tall man said. "I was hoping you might have brought me what Rory stole from me."

"What did he steal?" Stephanie asked. "If you tell me, maybe I can help you find it."

Carlos Diego sighed loudly. "I don't think so, Miss Ryan. That isn't how I do business. You see, I'd hoped that you were coming to me in good faith. While you were hiking here, I told Rory that you had eluded that agent in your house and were going to deal with me directly. I told Rory that perhaps I would end his suffering swiftly if you brought me back my property. But if that isn't the case, then I'm afraid Rory is going to die a slow and painful death."

Stephanie fought against the fear that threatened to overwhelm her. She'd made this trek knowing that Diego was a dangerous man, capable of anything. She'd decided to negotiate for Rory's life. Now wasn't the time to lose her nerve.

"I want to help you," she said. "I want to give you what you want. But I can't unless I know what it is."

Diego stepped into the light where she could clearly see him. His features were classically handsome, but his eyes were like dark holes. "Maybe Rory will tell you what he took."

Rory's only answer was a groan.

"Plenty, perhaps you can make Rory tell his lovely fiancée what he took from me."

The big man who'd captured her walked over to Rory. He drew back his foot and kicked Rory in the stomach. The sound of the blow almost made Stephanie throw up.

"Stop!" She rushed forward and dropped down beside Rory. In the glare of the headlights she could see the blood that had soaked the dirt beneath him. His face was bloodied and bruised where he'd been beaten. Why had she ever thought she could negotiate with men like these? She'd gravely underestimated Diego and his men.

"Let Rory go and I'll find whatever it is you want and give it to you."

Both men laughed. "I don't think that sounds like much of a bargain for us, Miss Ryan."

"I won't help you unless you let Rory go. He's hurt. He needs a doctor."

"I can make it so he's out of pain. Permanently," Diego said, a dark edge in his voice. "Now give me the microchip. I know you must have brought it with you. You couldn't be so naive as to come here without it."

"I don't know what you're talking about. Rory never told me anything about his business. I thought he was a pilot, a charter pilot." She was talking too fast, but she didn't care. She had to keep talking. Maybe Johnny was out there. Maybe he'd actually come to the rescue. She had to give him time to reach her. She hadn't walked into Diego's camp totally unprepared, but she was outnumbered. She needed Johnny's help. That was her only chance to escape alive and maybe even save Rory.

"But now you know the truth, don't you?" Carlos asked. "Johnny Kreel has told you about Rory, hasn't he?"

"Johnny told me that Rory wasn't just a pilot." She had to tread carefully. "He told me that Rory worked for you and that he took something that was yours. Johnny said you wouldn't rest until you got it back."

"Is that all Johnny told you?" Diego asked.

She nodded. "That's all. He didn't tell me anything else."

"And did Johnny search for this thing that Rory stole?"

"He did. But he didn't find it."

"You wouldn't lie to me, would you?"

"I have no reason to lie, because I don't know what you want. All I want is for you to leave me and my ranch alone. You burned my barn and you let a very expensive stallion loose. Running Horse Ranch is my livelihood. I'll give you what's yours, if you tell me what it is, and if you'll promise to leave me alone."

"Well, of course," Diego said, and in the headlights of the vehicle his smile looked like something on a cadaver. "I think we can reach a deal, Miss Ryan."

"Good," she said. "Then cut Rory loose. He's injured and can't get away. There's no need for him to be tied up."

Diego turned to the large man. "Plenty, cut Rory's bonds. His fiancée is unhappy that he's tied up."

"Certainly," Plenty said. He brought a knife from a

sheath at his belt. In two seconds the wicked blade sliced through the air. Rory screamed.

Stephanie cried out, but her cry was drowned out in the laughter of the two men.

Chapter Sixteen

When his breathing was under control, Johnny moved stealthily to the front door of Rupert Casper's ranch house. The place looked like something out of a movie set—a huge, rambling log cabin and a series of barns and out-buildings. From what Johnny could tell, the place was im-maculately maintained.

The bunkhouse was quiet, but someone was up in the main house. Johnny had to get closer to be sure who it was. He'd never bothered to ask Stephanie if Casper was married or single. It hadn't seemed pertinent at the time. Now he wished he knew a bit more about the man.

Johnny started closer to the house, and Familiar moved with him. The cat was like his shadow and, crazy as it seemed, Familiar gave him a sense of security.

Moving around the house, Johnny went to the lighted window and peered inside. Casper sat at a burnished mahogany table with another man. The two were deep in conversation. For some reason, watching them gave Johnny a creeping sense of foreboding.

But he had to use the telephone. He had to get a call in to Hance Bevins and get help for Stephanie.

"Wait here," he told Familiar. "Casper isn't going to be happy to see me, but he'd shoot you after what you did to his truck."

"Meow." Familiar's answer was barely audible.

When he started forward, the cat snagged him with a paw. Johnny could tell that Familiar, too, was having misgivings about approaching Rupert Casper for help. Something just wasn't right. What was Casper doing conducting a business meeting at four in the morning? Casper was up to something, but Johnny didn't have time to play around and determine what it was.

He went to the front door and knocked loudly. A light came on in the bunkhouse and the front door opened. A cowboy, already dressed for the day, stepped onto the porch. He lit a cigarette and watched Johnny.

Johnny knocked on the entry to the main house again.

The door finally opened, and Rupert Casper didn't bother to hide his surprise. "Trouble at Running Horse?" he asked.

"Do you have a landline for your phone?" Johnny asked. "We've got some reception problems and I need to make an important call."

"Must be an emergency to come over at four in the morning," Casper said. His tone was friendly, a fact that made Johnny even more suspicious. Had a neighbor shown up to use a phone at 4:00 a.m., Johnny would have suspected an emergency, but he would have been concerned rather than amused. Not Rupert Casper. In fact, he seemed pleased.

"If I could borrow your phone, I'll be on my way." Johnny had no intention of telling him anything.

"I'm sorry. No landlines in this area. Not populated enough to warrant any," Casper said. He used his thumb and forefinger to rub his chin. "No cell reception, either. Around here it's unreliable at best. Sorry I can't help." He started to shut the door but stopped. "How's Black Jack doing? This trouble doesn't involve him, does it? I warned Miss Ryan that he was dangerous. If she's hurt, it's her own fault."

Johnny wanted to punch him in the face. It was clear that Casper knew there was some kind of trouble at Running Horse, and he was gloating over it. But why? What did he stand to gain from misfortune at Stephanie's ranch?

"Could I borrow a vehicle? I need to drive where I can get phone service. I'll bring it right back."

"I'm sorry, Mr. Kreel. My vehicles are down, too. Damnedest thing, wouldn't you say?" Rupert Casper smiled. He softly closed the door.

It took a moment for Johnny to accept that Casper was such a lowlife that he'd deliberately turn his back on a neighbor in trouble. But that's exactly what he'd done. And he'd done it with a smile on his face.

Johnny stepped off the porch and into the thin moonlight. He could kick the door down, punch Casper out, try the phone or find some keys, but he'd never get away when the cowboys and staff on the ranch came after him. That would do Stephanie no good. He couldn't allow himself to imagine what was happening to her.

Over at the bunkhouse the cowboy on the porch tossed his cigarette to the ground and stepped out to crush it in the dirt. "Hey," he called softly.

Desperate, Johnny walked over. "I need to make a phone call," he said.

"You're the guy helping Ms. Ryan, aren't you?"

Johnny's fists clenched. "What of it?"

"I'm Jasper Platt. I hear Casper's got a burn on bad for

the two of you. I heard him talking to the guy who keeps coming by here about how much he wants to take you both down a notch." The cowboy made a sound of amusement. "Whatever you did to him, it stuck in his craw. He hates the two of you."

Immediately, Johnny understood that the man standing in front of him loathed Rupert Casper as much as he did. "Jasper, I don't think much of a man who beats a horse to the point that he turns rank and develops an uncontrollable fear of humans."

"Yeah, I heard what he did to Black Jack. Too bad the horse didn't kill him. Casper's a self-righteous badass." The cowboy shook out another smoke. "I'd lend you a truck, but I don't have one. But I do have a fine mare. You can ride her about two miles east and get perfect cell reception. Make your call and bring her back."

Johnny grasped the man's shoulder. "Thank you."

"Hey, anybody who gets under Casper's skin like you did must have some good in him."

"Could I ask a favor?" Another idea had formed full-blown in Johnny's head. It was crazy to trust someone he'd never met before, but he had no choice, really. A four-mile round trip ride on horseback would take half an hour or better at high speed—and that was time Stephanie might not have.

"You can ask. Won't guarantee I'll do it."

"Could I get you to take that ride and make a call for me? It's serious. Government business."

The cowboy hesitated. "This sounds like you're getting ready to play me for a fool. Government business. That's generally a ticket straight to the hot place."

Johnny couldn't stop the smile. Cowboys were an independent breed with little use for the federal government or law enforcement types. They minded their own business, and when it was necessary, they took care of people who treated them wrong. "There's a killer loose in this area, and he's taken Ms. Ryan hostage. I'm trying to save her. If you'd make that call, it would be a big help."

Suspicion dropped from the cowboy's face. "You're serious about this."

Johnny pulled his badge from his back pocket and flipped it open. "I'm relying on you to keep this to yourself. But if you'll make this call…" He handed him his cell phone. "Just hit the talk button and when someone answers, tell them Johnny Kreel needs full backup. Choppers, ground support, surveillance, everything. Make sure they understand *full backup*. Tell them Carlos Diego is in the area and has taken two hostages."

"Two?"

Johnny didn't have time to explain. "That's right. Can you do that?"

"Let me saddle up."

"Can I borrow another horse?"

The cowboy thought. "Take Gibb's horse. He left Rascal here until he got a new job. He won't mind."

"Thanks."

They hurried into the barn.

MY MAMA ALWAYS WARNED ME *that eavesdropping would come to no good end. Now I know what she meant. Johnny is getting a horse from Jasper Platt. A horse. Great. Somehow I knew it would eventually come down to this. Fate would never let me escape at least one horseback ride. And the beast's name is Rascal. How appropriate.*

Here comes Johnny out of the barn. The little horse is moving out calmly. And Johnny has stopped and is leaning down, waiting for me to leap into his arms.

Here goes nothing!

I'm onboard and we're setting off at a gallop. Jasper is tearing off in the opposite direction on another horse. Now the front door of the ranch house is flying open to reveal Rupert Casper standing in the doorway like doom. He's very unhappy, and I suspect Jasper Platt is going to be looking for a new job when he returns.

Hey, what's going on here? Another man is joining Casper on the porch. They're running to get in a truck. They're following us?

What the dickens? Why would Rupert Casper care if we borrowed a horse that isn't his?

Johnny is aware that we've picked up a tail and he's doing what any good, insane cowboy would do. He's cutting across the range. I certainly hope this horse knows how to dodge holes. A fall at this speed would kill us all.

The best I can do is close my eyes and hang on to the saddle with all four claws. Miss Cowgirl, we're on the way—if we live long enough to get there to rescue you.

Oh, crap, that looks like a small ravine ahead. About three feet wide. And as far as I can see in the moonlight, it looks deep. Rascal isn't slowing. Horses see pretty well at night, or so I've been told. Can this horse not see that we're going to fall into a gully?

Oh, the horse sees it, and so does Johnny. But he isn't going to slow up. This is what I hate about riding horses. We're going to jump! Oh, great tigress, watch out for your fine black cat!

Whew! We're on the other side. And behind us Casper

is still coming at ninety miles an hour. I begin to see the brilliance of Johnny's plan to jump the ravine.

One, two, three—whammo! Rupert Casper must not have seen the ravine in time to stop, and let me just say that a truck cannot leap a three-foot divide. Johnny has slowed long enough to check out the damage, and it is superb. Casper and his cohort are jammed halfway in the ravine. If they move too much, the truck may get dislodged and fall all the way in. I hope they're sweating bullets. I have no idea why they were chasing us, but we can find that out later.

Ah, there is a keen sense of justice at work here. No time to enjoy the spectacle, though. We're off to save Miss Cowgirl.

RORY HAD SLIPPED into an uneasy sleep filled with twitches and tremors. Stephanie knew some of it was from the cold ground but most of it derived from his injuries. She moved closer to him, trying to use her body warmth to keep him alive.

The blood loss from the gunshot wound wouldn't normally be enough to kill him, but the big man called Plenty had really worked Rory over, with his fists and his knife. Rory had some broken ribs, at the very least. His breathing sounded as if the damage might be more severe. Without medical attention, he would surely die.

For the moment, Carlos Diego had decided to leave the two of them alone. He'd told them he would wait until light so Rory could watch what he intended to do. This was only a respite, Stephanie knew. Diego intended to kill Rory no matter what, and probably she would die, too.

Her hardheadedness had put her in a very bad spot indeed. She should have listened to Johnny.

When she thought of Johnny, she was nearly overwhelmed by emotion. Lying on the ground beside a man who was destined to die, if not dying already, she realized how she'd cheated herself.

She'd had one memorable night in Johnny's arms. That was all. Some lucky folks spent a lifetime sleeping next to the person they loved. For her, that time had been all too brief. Even as she'd made love to Johnny, her heart had known how much she felt for him, how deep and how quickly her love for him had grown.

He'd stepped into the void left by Rory and he'd filled it completely—and offered so much more. By contrast, the love she'd thought she felt for Rory was a poor imitation. Because of her own stubborn nature, she'd learned this too late.

The man beside her shook with a chill, and she pressed closer to him, but her thoughts were on Johnny. She allowed herself time to visualize him in splendid detail. He was ruggedly handsome, and she loved the way he moved. Even though he'd lied to her repeatedly, Stephanie knew he'd only done so to protect her. Especially from the knowledge that Rory was alive.

Johnny had gained nothing from withholding that. He'd done it because he'd known how deeply the truth would cut her.

She remembered the way he'd jumped into the round pen and boosted her out of Black Jack's way. He'd risked his own life to save hers. And then he'd won the stallion over.

Just as he'd won her over. Johnny had a way of touching her that moved her to a degree she'd never experienced. His touch communicated his courage and kindness. He'd tamed her much as he had Black Jack. All in all, he was a pretty remarkable man.

Rory moaned softly, and she felt his forehead. He was

burning up with fever. The gunshot had likely gotten infected, and she'd carry the burden of his death for as long as she lived. Which probably wasn't going to be much longer.

Judging by the angle of the moon, dawn wasn't far off. In a short time, the east would show the first pinky-gray tones of day. Once that happened, Diego was going to kill Rory and then her. Or maybe he'd kill her first in an attempt to get Rory to tell him where the microchip was.

But she had a tiny surprise. She'd come on a fool's errand and she acknowledged that her actions were ill-advised and hardheaded, but the fat lady hadn't sung yet. Stephanie had learned something very valuable in the last two days. She was capable of killing to protect the things she loved.

DAWN BEGAN TO BRIGHTEN the eastern horizon. Johnny had ground-tied Rascal in the safety of a small canyon. The horse had a bit of grass and the trickle of a small creek to drink from, and he was also far enough away that any noise he made couldn't be heard by the men in the camp below. Johnny had climbed to high ground, where he could watch Carlos Diego start the day.

It was remarkable that Diego had been so careless. The Colombian was known for his security and intelligence. Therefore, he must have an ace up his sleeve. He didn't believe Johnny would risk attacking his encampment because Stephanie would certainly be killed in the melee.

It was a tough predicament. As daybreak illuminated the scene below him, he could make out Plenty, stretching and scratching. Carlos Diego, too, rolled out of a bedroll. Two other henchmen had also risen for the day. And at last he saw Stephanie, pressed against Rory. The sight was like a knife blade to his gut, but he ignored it. If Stephanie were still in love with Rory, if she could forgive him for all he'd done, Johnny would walk away. He'd known when he went to Running Horse Ranch that Stephanie had accepted a marriage proposal from Rory. She obviously had strong feelings for him.

The night they'd spent together, while the most significant event of his life, had been stolen time. He and Stephanie had come together as two desperate people fueled by the knowledge that their lives were in danger. How well he knew the intoxication of danger. And Stephanie had awakened from the spell of it and made her choice. She'd gone after her fiancé to rescue him—even at the risk of her own life. While Johnny didn't like it, he also wouldn't fight it.

He had to stop thinking about Stephanie and his feelings for her. Those very feelings could get them all killed if he didn't keep them in check. A good agent never let emotion interfere with his decisions. He'd gone through years of training to learn how to turn his feelings off. And that was exactly what he intended to do.

Staring down at the camp, he observed the scene without emotion. Rory looked like hell. Aside from the gunshot wound, someone had beaten him severely. Stephanie looked unharmed, but she was clearly concerned about Rory. He could tell by how she touched his forehead and leaned over him.

Had Stephanie not taken it upon herself to rush to Rory's rescue, Johnny would have had a number of better options to rescue Rory. Now, though, any action he took would result in the death of Rory and/or Stephanie. He was an excellent shot, but he couldn't pick off Diego, Plenty and their two other accomplices before they killed Rory or Stephanie.

But that was exactly what he had to do. He'd have one

chance at this, and if he messed it up, Stephanie would likely die.

As he watched, Plenty walked over and kicked Rory hard. Stephanie rose up to protest, and Plenty slapped her.

Johnny focused his shot through the rifle, centering on Plenty's forehead. He wanted to pull the trigger. He itched to pull it. Plenty was a cold-blooded murderer who took pleasure in inflicting pain on helpless victims. His death would be a boon to the world.

But it wasn't time. Not yet. Everything had to be perfect. If only he could alert Stephanie that he was there and that help from Omega would surely be on the way soon.

As Johnny watched, Plenty went to Rory and pulled him to his knees. The other two henchmen gathered around Rory and Stephanie. Carlos Diego made a show of preparing a cup of coffee, his back turned to the others. But when he turned around, things would heat up, Johnny knew.

The endgame had begun.

Chapter Seventeen

Stephanie stepped between Plenty and Rory. Her heart was thudding with fear, but she couldn't let Plenty kill Rory right in front of her.

"Move," Plenty said. He lifted a hand in warning that he meant to knock her out of his way.

In the morning light Stephanie was even more afraid of him than she'd been the night before. He was huge, at least six foot eight and two hundred and fifty pounds. None of it was fat. His black hair was slicked back in a ponytail, and a large scar ran from the corner of his right eye down to his lip. The scar tissue had pulled his face into a permanent grimace. He smiled as he saw her reaction to his appearance.

"Let me talk to Rory," she said, hoping to buy some time. "He'll tell me where this thing you want is hidden."

Plenty glanced beyond her and she was sure he was checking with Carlos Diego. Apparently, the boss man agreed to give her a chance to get the information from Rory, because Plenty shrugged. "Talk. But make it fast. We can make him talk without you."

"If that were true, you'd know where to look," she pointed out. "You haven't been able to beat it out of him so far."

"Talk," Plenty said gruffly.

She nodded and turned to face Rory, who swayed on his knees as if he might collapse back into the dirt.

The fever was higher, and Stephanie wondered if Rory would understand the dire situation they were in. He looked around, but she couldn't be certain the circumstances registered with him. If he wasn't able to play along... She couldn't begin to think of what might happen to them both.

She put a hand on his shoulder and dropped to her knees in front of him. "Rory, what did you hide at the ranch?" She used her free hand to hook her hair behind an ear, revealing one of the earrings.

He glanced at her, confusion on his heated face. "Stephanie?" he said, as if he wasn't certain it was her.

"What did you hide at Running Horse Ranch?" she asked calmly. "Tell me what it was and where you hid it, Rory, or they're going to kill us."

She made a point of pushing her hair behind her ear again. This time Rory's vision caught on the earring. She saw his focus sharpen and awareness light his face. She shifted her body so that Plenty couldn't see. "Tell me what's at the ranch," she said again, emphasizing *ranch*.

Rory took a ragged breath. He swayed on his knees, and she reached out to support him. "The list of agents," he said softly. "I took it from Capricorn, Diego's contact."

Stephanie's gaze never left Rory's, but she could feel Plenty and even Carlos Diego pressing closer. "What was on the list?" she asked.

"Names. Places. Dates. The Middle Eastern operation." Rory reached up and touched her hair, his finger tracing down one of the earrings. "It's worth a whole lot of money."

It was the signal Stephanie had been waiting for. Despite

his injuries and the fever, Rory was lucid enough to understand. He would play along. He knew she had the microchip, but he would divert part of Diego's forces back to the ranch to search for it.

"Tell me where the information is located at the *ranch,* Rory. Mr. Diego is eventually going to get it, and he's going to hurt us both until he does. We might as well give it to him. Where did you hide it at the *ranch?*"

"I can't tell." Rory caressed her cheek, and Stephanie clearly saw the regret in his eyes. "I'm sorry I dragged you into this. I didn't mean to. I was going back to the ranch to get the— I never meant to put you in danger. Never."

"Can the soap opera," Plenty said, walking closer. "Where's the microchip? What does it look like?"

Rory shook his head. "She doesn't know anything. Let her go and I'll tell you."

Plenty grasped Stephanie's hair. He jerked her head back exposing her throat. She felt the blade of a knife.

"Where is the microchip?" he asked again.

"Let her go," Rory said calmly.

Plenty shoved Stephanie so hard she fell forward. When she came down on her knees, she put her hands on Rory's chest in a supplicating gesture. "Tell him what he wants to know. Please."

"I can't." Rory gave her an imperceptible nod. "Diego can't get the information. He'll sell it—"

Stephanie sensed the approach of Plenty and knew he'd hurt Rory again. Rory was playing his role too well. She whirled around. "Give me a minute, okay? I can make him tell me where it is."

"See that you do," Diego said as he walked up. "And be quick. Daylight isn't our friend." He glanced around.

"Your houseguest will be trying to contact his superiors and bring in help."

"Johnny can't get help. There's no phone reception, the Internet connection is destroyed and our vehicles are disabled. There's not even a horse there he can ride," Stephanie pointed out to him. "The only place within five miles he can go is Rupert Casper's."

"That's not really an option." Diego made a dismissive gesture with his hand. "Casper plays for our team now."

Stephanie was stunned, and she didn't bother to hide it. "Casper? Why would he help you?"

Carlos lifted one shoulder. "He wants your property, and he'll be able to buy it for a dime on the dollar once this is done."

Stephanie clamped down on her temper. She'd deal with Rupert Casper when she finished with Carlos and Plenty. But first she needed Rory to help her. She turned back to him. "Where is the information? What does it look like?"

"In the cabin," Rory gasped. He swayed and Stephanie caught him and helped him into a sitting position on the ground.

"Where?" she pressed. "Tell me, Rory. We have to try to save ourselves."

"Tell her!" Plenty pushed the barrel of a gun into Rory's temple. "Tell her or I'll splatter your brains all over her and we'll take that ranch apart board by board."

Rory finally nodded, as if he'd conceded. "In the fishing tackle box. I tied it into a fishing lure," Rory said. "A yellow sally. It's a tiny microchip."

Stephanie held her breath. If Diego didn't kill them both now, her plan might work.

"Where is that tackle box?" the leader demanded. "Tell me."

Stephanie nodded. "It's in the utility room in the cabin, where the washer and dryer are. There's a cabinet above the dryer. It's there." She licked her dry lips. If she'd ever wanted to bluff her way out of a situation, now was the time.

"Kill them," Diego said to Plenty. He waved toward his two gunmen. "You two, drive to the ranch and get the tackle box."

Gun drawn, Plenty came toward Stephanie. She held up a hand. "Rory is delirious. You should find the tackle box before you kill him. What if the micro-whatever isn't there? I don't know where it is. Believe me, Johnny and I searched everywhere for it."

Plenty smiled, an action that pulled the scar on his face into a distorted mask. "Maybe we should keep Rory alive, but we don't have to keep you alive. Can I have her, Boss?"

Stephanie didn't move. Pleading would do no good. Carlos Diego wasn't moved by pleas, and a show of desperation would only excite Plenty. Johnny had been right to caution her about Plenty. He was a dangerously disturbed, sociopathic killer. Johnny had been right about a lot of things. She felt a dull ache in her chest at the thought of him and all she'd given up to rescue Rory. She'd grieve the loss of Johnny later. Right now, she had to survive.

For a tense moment, Diego considered Plenty's request. Stephanie watched as two of the gunmen got in one of the vehicles and tore off, heading toward the ranch.

Now Diego would decree her fate, and if her hand was

forced, she'd make her play. Her fingers slipped down to her shin.

"Leave her," Diego said. He pointed toward the disappearing vehicle. "When they return, she's yours."

Stephanie inhaled. It felt as if she'd been holding her breath for days. Two down—two to go. But one of the two was the most deadly man she'd ever come across.

"We should just kill her," Plenty grumbled. "She's only going to be trouble."

She spoke before Diego reconsidered his decree. "Thank you, Mr. Diego. I can get through to Rory when no one else can." She ignored Plenty, hoping he would grow tired of hovering over her. She wasn't ready to take him on. Not yet. But soon.

JOHNNY WATCHED THE SCENE play out and held his breath. When Rory stroked Stephanie's hair and face, he ground his teeth, but he never stopped watching.

He hated that Stephanie had a past with Rory. He hated that she still cared enough for him to risk her life. But he also admired her for loving deeply enough to look beyond Rory's betrayals. She was a rare person. He'd give a lot to have someone love him that much.

Stephanie showed such tenderness to Rory, who was obviously injured. Johnny saw her push her hair back behind her ears, revealing the earrings, and he suddenly understood what she was doing.

The full scope of Stephanie's plan came to him in a rush. It was, possibly, the only way to save Rory, the ranch and the vital information. If it didn't work, both Stephanie and Rory would die.

When the two gunmen left the campsite in a cloud of

dust, Johnny had to hand it to Stephanie. She'd evened the odds—two against two. And she had to believe that he and Familiar would be out here, trying to figure out a rescue plan. Did she sense him? She was too smart to look up. But he hoped that she knew he was there, ready to back her play.

From his vantage point, there was a possibility that he could actually kill Plenty and Carlos before either man fired a shot. It was a slim chance, but it might work. He was a crackerjack shot and had proven it more than once in the field. But never before had the life of the woman he loved hung in the balance. If he missed—if he couldn't kill both Plenty and Carlos—Stephanie would die.

Beside him, Familiar studied the scene. The cat had been unnaturally quiet, as if he, too, weighed the odds of any action.

Suddenly, Stephanie stood and walked to Plenty. She seemed to engage him in conversation. Johnny watched, reading the cock of her head, the way she held herself. She didn't appear afraid, which was the smartest thing she could do. Plenty fed off the fear he inspired in his victims. But what was she doing?

When she turned and gave a shrill whistle, Johnny was dumbfounded. She put two fingers in her mouth and let loose a second piercing sound. Johnny heard it clearly from his perch. Familiar even sat up. The sound hit the foothills and bounced back.

Plenty slapped the back of Stephanie's head, almost knocking her down. Johnny jumped to his feet, but Familiar's claws dug into him, reminding him that giving his position away would help no one.

Damn. He itched to put a bullet in Plenty's forehead. The man was a brute and a bully. That was the ticket. Just blow him away. Once he fired the first shot, he had to have a clear shot at Diego, too. The first thing Diego would do would be to shoot Stephanie and Rory.

Johnny forced his body to relax. As he watched, Rory lurched to his feet and stumbled toward Plenty and Stephanie. Even from a distance, Johnny could see how badly injured his old friend was. Yet he was trying to protect Stephanie. A day late and a dollar short, as far as Johnny was concerned. Rory had put Stephanie's life on the line, and for what? Money?

Now wasn't the time for anger, though. Johnny sighted the rifle on Plenty. Just as he was about to squeeze the trigger, Plenty grabbed Stephanie by the hair for the second time and pulled her into his arms. One beefy forearm circled her waist, and he lifted her.

The blood pulsed in Johnny's temples as he aimed. If he was off by a hair, he would hit Stephanie. Where the hell was Bevins and the backup? He needed a show of force. Johnny eased off the trigger. He didn't have a clean shot.

Carlos Diego leaned against the remaining SUV, watching the struggle without taking part. He waved a hand at Plenty, who dropped Stephanie as if she were a sack of oats.

Now Johnny had a clear shot at the big man, but just as he started to squeeze the trigger, Diego pulled a gun and pointed it at Stephanie.

And with that, the odds changed out of Johnny's favor. Somehow Stephanie had gotten rid of two of Diego's men, but he couldn't risk a shot. Not with her life hanging in the balance.

As he lay on the ground, his whole body tensed to take a shot, he felt a rumble. His first thought was that a mild earthquake was rumbling through the Black Hills, but that was ridiculous. It took him a moment to realize what he was feeling, but when he did, he turned to Familiar.

"It's the horses," he said.

The black cat was already focused to the west. Familiar had sensed the approach of the herd before Johnny had even felt it.

The thud of the hooves grew stronger. Carlos and Plenty hadn't yet felt it—or if they had they didn't recognize a stampede. Johnny looked to the west just in time to see the first horse top a rise.

Black Jack, as wild and free as any range stallion that had ever run, came over the hill. The morning sun struck his black coat, creating the effect of lightning rippling along the horse. Behind him were Flicker, Layla and the rest of the Running Horse Ranch herd. And behind them came twenty head of wild mustangs.

Johnny was speechless. He watched in awe as the horses poured over the rise and aimed straight for Stephanie and Rory and the others. It was as if Stephanie had called them to her in her moment of need.

Diego was caught off guard and momentarily distracted. Both he and Plenty stopped, focused entirely on the herd. Neither had yet comprehended the danger. But Stephanie had. She grasped Rory and forced him to his feet. Half carrying and half supporting him, she moved toward the SUV.

She opened the back door and shoved Rory inside.

Johnny waited for her to get in, but she didn't. Instead, she reached into her boot and brought out something that glinted in the sun.

Johnny found himself rising to his feet. He wanted to yell, to tell Stephanie to get into the SUV, but she couldn't hear him.

The horses bore down on the campsite. Too late, Plenty and his boss recognized the danger. Plenty raised his pistol, aiming directly at Black Jack. Stephanie dove at him, the knife she held flashing in the morning light as she slashed across his arm.

There was the sound of a gunshot and then another as Johnny jumped up and ran toward Stephanie. And then the campsite was covered in horses and a cloud of dust.

RUN, JOHNNY, RUN! I'm right behind you even though that horseback ride jarred every bone in my body. No time now to sing the cow-cat's complaint. This is our moment for action.

The horses are the perfect cover for us to get in there and take care of Carlos Diego and his right-hand man. Whoever would have thought that black demon horse would show up when he was needed most. I take back all the bad things I thought about him in the beginning. He is not the spawn of Satan. He is not a rogue. He is not destined for a dog-food can.

He is, in fact, a godsend.

But who can see anything in all that dust? Where is Miss Cowgirl? And more important, where is that big man with the lust to kill? I want him for my own. If I were the kind of cat to take trophies, I'd consider putting him in a cage in the backyard as an example of a biped gone bad. But my fondest hope is that he ends up in a cage and the South Dakotan government will have to feed and shelter him. I have better things to do with my time.

The horses have created such a ruckus, I'm not certain where to go. My best thought is to hide under the SUV until the dust clears. Then I have a fantasy of jumping on that lowlife's head and tearing his ears off. Talk about ride 'em, cowboy!

Johnny disappeared in the mayhem. The only thing I can do is wait for a chance to help. And hope Miss Cowgirl isn't hurt.

And where in hell is the backup that Johnny called for? I'm going to write a letter about how my tax dollars aren't working for me!

STEPHANIE FELT THE BLADE of the knife strike the bone of Plenty's upper arm. Because of that she wasn't prepared for the backhand he struck her with. Obviously impervious to pain, he hit her so hard that she spun, and in the dust raised by the horses she lost her bearings. She couldn't see anything, while all around her were the thundering bodies of the horses.

She'd meant to call them, but she'd never imagined that they would come into the camp and actually storm Diego and Plenty. But they did, Black Jack at the lead.

Rory was safe in the SUV, or as safe as he could be with the serious injuries he'd sustained. Now she had to find a weapon and finish what she'd started with Diego and Plenty. If she could stay alive another five minutes, Johnny would come. She felt him close. She couldn't explain it, but she knew he was trying to help her.

Given her druthers, she'd collect Rory and the horses and leave, but Diego would never let her. She knew that. In the hour or so she'd spent in the company of Carlos Diego, she'd come to believe everything Johnny had warned her about. Diego was a cold-blooded killer, just like his burly hired hand.

Somewhere in the melee of horses and dust were

weapons, and she needed something more than a knife. Plenty had taken the Glock and the rifle from her, but she couldn't remember where they were. In her mind she retraced the sequence of events until she recalled that the guns were in the backseat of the SUV. They were there with Rory. All she had to do was get there, get her hands on one of them and kill Diego and Plenty. Then she could drive Rory to the hospital.

She turned slowly, straining to see through the dust. At last she saw the vehicle, and she went toward it. The back door opened easily, and she reached inside and found the Glock on the floorboard.

Rory lay slumped in the seat. For a moment she thought he was dead, but she touched him and felt warm skin. Too warm due to the fever. But he was alive, and if she got him to the hospital fast enough, he might make it.

Grasping the Glock, she eased out of the car and closed the door. Flicker whizzed by her, almost knocking the gun from her hand and her into the dirt. When she recovered, she turned to search for Plenty—and found herself looking right into the barrel of the gun he held at her forehead.

Chapter Eighteen

Johnny was two hundred yards behind the horses when they swept into the campsite. From that short distance, it looked to him as if the herd was staging an organized charge against Diego and Plenty. Impossible, but that's what it appeared to be. And Black Jack was the ringmaster of the show.

The stallion was magnificent. He spun and reared and whinnied, and the other horses clustered around him, hooves stamping the ground hard enough to create chaos and confusion.

Though Johnny was amazed by the stallion's actions, he had no time to ponder them. He had to get Stephanie safely out of that campsite. And Rory, too.

And the earrings.

Somehow, the microchip had fallen to his last priority. Which told him it was time to leave the business. Even though Stephanie still loved Rory, she was Johnny's primary focus. Maybe he would never have her, but he certainly wasn't going to let her die. If she chose to forgive Rory and stay with him, so be it.

All that could be dealt with later. For now, he had to

concentrate on his goals and on staying alive and rescuing Stephanie.

The camp was a whirlwind of dust, stirred by the horses as they ran madly back and forth. They could easily have swept through the camp and continued on, but they were running in circles, moving in and out, creating confusion and a cloud of dirt that was impenetrable.

Johnny entered the clash with his handgun in one hand and the rifle in the other. Familiar darted ahead of him, disappearing into the fracas.

Stephanie had been moving toward the SUV when Johnny last saw her, and he dashed in that direction. He couldn't see anything. He ran blind.

When he finally discerned the outline of the car, he slowed. The hulking frame of Plenty came out of the dusty fog, and Johnny saw the deadly gunman moving toward the SUV—toward the place he'd last seen Stephanie.

Johnny couldn't stop the surge of concern that swept through him. The only thing that kept Plenty in check was Diego, and Diego had disappeared in the stampede. There was a good chance he was dead, and if that was the case, Plenty would have no compunction about hurting Stephanie.

Three shots came from Johnny's immediate right. The scream of an injured horse sounded close, but Johnny couldn't tell which equine had been hurt. "Damn," he muttered, galvanized into action by the shots. Johnny didn't think Plenty had fired, so that meant his boss was alive and he had a gun. The criminal mastermind had injured one of the horses. As soon as Stephanie was safe, Johnny vowed he'd find Carlos and make him pay. For a lot of things.

The thick dust began to settle as Johnny saw the horses

head due east. They'd raced on to the scene, giving him a chance to get into the campsite unobserved. The cover they'd given him would be lost if he didn't act fast.

If he could get Stephanie out of the camp, then he could focus on Plenty and Diego.

His heart thumped painfully when he saw Plenty at the SUV. He held a gun, the barrel touching Stephanie's head.

"Plenty!" Johnny bolted forward. "Hey! Plenty!" He never saw Carlos, and he was unprepared for the blow that landed on his temple. He tumbled to the ground, poleaxed but still conscious.

Shaking his head to clear it, Johnny found himself staring at a nightmare. Plenty still held a gun to Stephanie's forehead and had an evil smile on his face.

"She's a dead woman," Plenty said, "and then I'll take care of you and the traitor."

It seemed as if everything grew totally silent. All sound fled. Except for the click as Plenty cocked the hammer on the revolver. He meant to kill Stephanie right there.

Johnny rolled toward Plenty, gained his feet and came up with his gun aimed at the big killer. His finger was on the trigger when Diego stepped in front of him.

"Put it down," Diego said. He pressed the barrel of a handgun to Johnny's heart. "Now."

Johnny cast one look at Stephanie, frozen in a tableau with Plenty. The expression on her face told him she realized the desperation of her plight. Once he lowered his gun, they were as good as dead. He looked around the campsite, hoping for some advantage.

The dust had dissipated, and Johnny could hear and feel the retreating hoofbeats of the horses. They'd all fled, and by now were at least a mile away. Except for Black Jack.

The black stallion stumbled toward Stephanie. Blood ran down his front legs and his chest was coated in dust that had clotted in his blood.

"No!" Stephanie saw the stallion. "He's hurt." She tried to move past Plenty toward the horse.

Plenty raised the gun, ready to bring it across her face. Johnny tensed, prepared to intervene, but Diego pressed the barrel hard into his chest.

"You can't save her," Diego said. "You can't even save yourself. Soon my men will be back with the microchip and you will die. I think I'll let Plenty have his fun with you. He's earned it."

Before Johnny could react, a small black form shot out from under the SUV. Familiar took one bounce and landed squarely on Plenty's face. With a shriek of fury, the cat raked his claws down the killer's eyes. For good measure, Familiar bit into the man's earlobe and tore as he jumped away.

Blinded by his own blood, Plenty raised his hands to his face. Diego was distracted, and Johnny spun and brought a foot up to kick him in the throat. He went down like a sack of bricks, gasping and struggling for air.

Johnny turned to help Stephanie, but he stopped. She was handling Plenty on her own. She brought her knee up sharply into his groin, and when he doubled over in pain, she used both fists to hammer the back of his neck. He dropped to the ground, writhing.

Johnny took no risks. He used his gun butt to make certain Carlos and Plenty were unconscious and would remain that way for a while. When the immediate danger was over, he went to Stephanie.

"Are you hurt?" he asked.

"No. But Black Jack is." She fought back her tears. "Rory's in the SUV. He's hurt, too."

"I'll see to Rory. You help the horse. He saved your life, you know."

"I know. He and Familiar." She frowned. "Where is that cat?"

They looked around to see Familiar sitting on the ground, his green gaze leveled at Black Jack. The stallion staggered, and Stephanie began pulling off her jacket.

"We've got to help Black Jack," she said as she hurried toward the horse.

A distant hum seemed to hover on the horizon. It took Johnny a minute to fully comprehend what the slight buzz of noise meant. The cavalry was finally on the way. It was the sound of a helicopter winging toward them.

AT FIRST, STEPHANIE couldn't figure out where Black Jack was injured. The blood seemed to be all over his neck and chest and legs. Her hands moved over him, pressing, seeking the wound with the hope of stopping the bleeding. If she didn't, he would die.

"Easy, boy," she whispered.

The stallion's muzzle pushed at her neck, a whisper-soft caress.

She couldn't lose him. Not now. He'd not only come around, he'd saved her life at the risk of his own.

Her fingers moved along his hide until at last she found the wound. The bullet had entered above his shoulder at the point where his neck began, and it appeared to have exited near his withers.

"Okay, fella," she said, trying to comfort and reassure him. A week ago she'd never have believed the stallion would trust her enough to let her take care of him. Now, though, he stood rock solid. His trust in her made her even more anxious. To win the heart of such an animal was the highest of honors, her grandfather had taught her. Now she fully understood what he'd meant.

Black Jack, like Familiar, was a rare creature. His presence in her life was a blessing from the Great Spirit, as her grandfather would say. Whether he'd been sent specifically to save her life or to teach her this valuable lesson, she couldn't say. It didn't matter. The only thing that counted now was to save him and then to make sure he was loved and honored for the rest of his days.

She held her jacket against the wound, applying as much pressure as she could. Black Jack stood stoically, never flinching or trying to evade her ministrations.

Johnny had opened the door of the SUV and was tending to Rory. She heard the helicopter drawing closer with every second. Help was on the way for Rory. In no time they could fly him to the hospital in Custer or even Rapid City. He'd get the best medical care. And then he'd face the consequences of his actions.

The thought left her feeling nothing. Rory had walked down a long and crooked path. She didn't want him to die, but she couldn't concern herself with the justice he now deserved.

The stallion's blood soaked through her jacket, but she kept pressing. If she didn't stanch the flow, he would bleed to death right there. She couldn't allow that. She wouldn't.

"How's Black Jack?" Johnny called as he helped Rory out of the car and stretched him on the ground.

"I can't apply enough pressure to stop the blood." She heard the panic in her own voice.

"I'll be there in a minute." He leaned over Rory, said something and pointed to the helicopter, which was landing fifty yards away. Then he raced to Stephanie's side.

His larger, stronger hands pressed on top of hers as he put his considerable strength into trying to seal the wound. Black Jack staggered again and almost dropped to his knees, but he managed to stand.

"What are we going to do?" Stephanie asked. She realized that she was crying. "He's dying right in front of me and I can't stop it."

Johnny pressed so hard she thought her hands would break. "Just keep pushing," Johnny whispered. "Push the blood back in. Visualize it."

She was surprised at the power in his voice, and she thought of her grandfather. Once he'd found a wolf caught in a leghold trap set by some illegal hunters. He'd opened the trap and released the wolf, and then he'd carried the young creature back to his ranch.

The wolf's leg had been badly damaged, and Running Horse was afraid the limb needed to be amputated. But he held off, and he sat with the wolf, rubbing the leg and talking to the wild creature.

"Dream of running," he said to the wolf. "Feel the dirt and grass beneath your paws. Feel the cool dew as you run." He'd talked to the wolf as he rubbed and manipulated the damaged leg.

And the wolf began to heal. In a matter of six weeks, the wolf was running with only the slightest trace of a limp. When Running Horse walked him into the woods to set him free, the wolf ran twenty yards away, and then he'd turned and howled before he disappeared into the wild.

"I couldn't have had the leg amputated," Running Horse

told her later. "A three-legged wolf can't survive in the wild, and to keep a wild creature captive is wrong."

"You would have put him down?" Stephanie had asked, shocked at the idea.

"To allow a creature to follow its nature is what we must do," he said. "For wolves as well as young girls."

It wasn't an answer, but Stephanie had taken the lesson as her grandfather intended. The power of healing had much to do with the belief that healing could occur. She saw the wound in Black Jack's glossy hide begin to close. She put every fiber of her being into seeing that.

Her eyes were closed and she felt the pressure of Johnny's hands lessen. When she opened her eyes, he was staring into the gaze of the stallion. Several men were running from the helicopter toward them. They all carried weapons, but two also carried medical bags. Johnny met the federal agents, and after a brief discussion, a team of agents headed toward the ranch to round up the thugs that had gone there. Johnny returned to her and Black Jack. He kissed her cheek. "The bleeding has stopped. If you want to fly to the hospital with Rory, I'll take care of Black Jack."

She only shook her head. "I'm staying," she said. "With you and the horse."

"Meow."

She looked down and Familiar was at her feet. He put a paw on her knee and rubbed against her leg.

"And Familiar," she added. "I'm staying with my guys."

"Whatever you think best," Johnny said before he turned and walked away.

Stephanie started to go after him, but she stopped. She followed him with her gaze until he began talking with a man who appeared to be in charge. The federal agent looked like a movie star playing the president.

IT'S NOT EVEN BREAKFAST TIME, and Rory has been loaded into a helicopter, along with a pair of handcuffed criminals. Carlos Diego finally regained consciousness, but he wasn't talking at all. And Plenty, that sicko, tried to wake up but Stephanie whacked him again. Probably not in the handbook of how to treat a federal prisoner, but no one seemed upset by Miss Cowgirl's actions. Except they had to lug the big oaf to the helicopter, which strained a few backs.

The medics that the Omega man brought along took a look at Black Jack. The bullet went through the muscle of his neck. It nicked some kind of major artery, but since the bleeding has stopped, the consensus is that Black Jack will heal just fine. They did a little suturing and bandaging. It's now a matter of getting him home.

The problem is that it's a long walk home, and Stephanie is afraid the wound will reopen en route. The medic did his best, but that part of a horse doesn't lend itself to stitches or bandaging. I guess a horse-to-horse transfusion is out of the question. At least out here on the range.

There's something eating at Johnny. He's too quiet. He went back to the canyon and retrieved Rascal, and he hasn't said a word since his return. And Miss Cowgirl looks like she's been run over by a tank. I did notice, though, that she's still wearing the earrings, yet no one has mentioned them and what they mean.

I wish I'd had a chance to grill Rory Sussex. What was he thinking when he took the microchip? A man like Carlos Diego doesn't allow people to steal from him. It's part of the code. So Rory had to know this would end badly for all involved. Especially Stephanie, who is truly an innocent in this mess.

Once again, another example of biped logic—as if such a thing exists. Talk about an oxymoron.

But it's head 'em up and move 'em out, get them doggies movin'. We're starting that long trek back to Running Horse Ranch. Black Jack is able to walk, but it's going to be a slow, drawn-out journey.

Chapter Nineteen

Stephanie closed the gate on the corral, checking the horses one more time to be sure they were all safe and accounted for. The sight of them, the golden October sun glinting off their hides, touched her heart in a profound way. They were home. Even Black Jack was eating hay in his round pen. His injuries weren't life-threatening. Hance Bevins had flown a specialist from Rapid City to examine the stallion. The gunshot, miraculously enough, would leave no serious aftereffects.

Even Tex had managed to survive his adventure on the open range with no serious repercussions. His leg would take a little longer to heal, but it would mend and he would be fine. The vet had advised giving him at least two days of rest before Johnny trailered him away.

Stephanie looked at the round pen where Johnny stood, one booted foot cocked on the lower rail, while he fed Black Jack some carrots.

They'd done the vet work and rounded up the horses, and Johnny still hadn't said a word to her. He was clearly upset, but all her attempts to explain her actions had been rebuffed.

Once he'd taken the earrings from her and turned them over to his boss, he hadn't even glanced her way.

"Meow."

She bent down to scoop Familiar into her arms. "Something tells me you're hungry," she whispered against his silky fur. "Well, so am I. What say we rustle up some grub and see if Johnny will come in and eat with us?"

Maybe he'd confront whatever was troubling him over some chow. If she trapped him in the kitchen, she might be able to force the issue. Out on the ranch, he simply came up with another chore to do so he could walk away from her.

"Me-ow!"

Familiar was adamant about food, so she carried him into the house. She selected trout that a friend had caught and put the fish in the sink to thaw. She had fixings for a fresh salad.

It would take a little while to prepare the food, so she found heavy whipping cream for Familiar. As he lapped up the cream, she stroked his fur.

"You aren't mad at me for trying to help Rory," she said. "I wish Johnny would understand."

Familiar glanced up, his eyes narrowing. Using one paw he delicately slapped the ring finger of her left hand.

Stephanie hesitated. Was the cat trying to tell her something?

"Meow!" Familiar put his paw on her finger and gently extended his claws. "Meow."

"My engagement ring?" she asked. She'd taken it off when she heard that Rory was dead. She hadn't known what to do with it. She'd put it in her jewelry box until the day someone had scattered the contents of the box on her bed. Then she'd absentmindedly placed it on her ring finger. "What about the ring?"

Familiar sighed deeply. He left the saucer of milk and

walked to the photograph of her and Rory. In the picture they both smiled into the camera as if they had the world by the tail.

"Meow." When Familiar had her full attention, he took his paw and pushed the photograph off the shelf and onto the floor. The glass shattered with a loud crash.

"Familiar! You did that deliberately." Stephanie's first reaction was annoyance. Then it slammed her like a ton of bricks. "But I don't love Rory. I'm beginning to wonder if I ever did."

Familiar jumped to the window and patted the glass.

She went to stand beside him. She had a clear view of Johnny as he stacked the charred debris of her barn. He was cleaning up. He'd told her he'd get as much done beforehand as he could.

Before what? She'd been afraid to ask him. Because she didn't want him to leave Running Horse Ranch.

His career as a federal agent was over. He hadn't told her that, but he didn't have to. She saw it clearly in the way he'd talked to his boss. In the fact that he hadn't asked her for the earrings but had waited for her to voluntarily give them up. In the way that he made it clear to everyone that her safety and the welfare of Black Jack and the other horses were his top priorities.

Yes, Johnny had shown her his heart.

And what had she shown him? She'd sneaked away in the dead of night to risk her life—and his—to save her ex-dead fiancé, a man who'd deliberately put her and everything she loved in harm's way.

"Oh, damn," she said, turning to toss the dish towel in her hand onto the table. "I'll be right back, Familiar," she said as she turned and ran out the door.

JOHNNY SLIPPED THROUGH the slats of the round pen and walked up to Black Jack. The stallion pushed him in the chest with his muzzle with enough force that Johnny stumbled.

"Good to see that you're feeling better," Johnny said, stroking the uninjured side of his neck. "You gave us a scare, big fella. And you also saved Stephanie's life. For that I owe you."

Black Jack whickered softly and shook his head.

"I don't think Rupert Casper's going to be troubling you anymore," Johnny said. "He's on his way to a stretch in a federal prison. Good things happen to bad people."

Black Jack nodded, snorting slightly.

"When Casper decided to help Diego and go against his own country, he made a bad choice. Of course, it's going to take him months to recover from the injuries he sustained in that wreck."

Snorting again, Black Jack nodded so vehemently his forelock landed in his eyes.

Johnny didn't mention the second man in the SUV that Casper ran into the ravine. He'd been killed on the spot. But he'd also been identified as an employee of Carlos Diego.

Both Diego and Plenty were in a federal facility in Washington, D.C.—so were Diego's two other henchmen. Johnny had received word that a full report was expected from him, and some testimony as to the course of events. But Hance Bevins had been pretty decent about the resignation Johnny turned in.

In a few weeks, Johnny would be free to start a new life— any kind of life he chose. He still had a law degree to fall back on. And he could live anywhere in the world he wanted.

The problem was he was standing on the plot of ground he wanted to make his home. But he'd never been the kind of guy who accepted second place. He wasn't a stand-in for Rory Sussex.

Rory was in the hospital at Custer with armed guards at his door 24/7. He was recovering and had regained consciousness.

Johnny checked his watch. He wanted to talk to Rory. They'd once been partners, closer than brothers. There were things to settle, and Johnny meant to have his answers.

"Johnny?"

Stephanie's voice was like salt in an open wound. He ignored her.

"Johnny, please. I want to talk to you."

"I don't want to talk to you," he said gruffly. "You made your choice clear. Leave it at that. When Tex is well, we'll be gone."

"You won't even give me a chance to explain?" she asked.

He faced her and saw the hurt in her golden-brown eyes. The sight almost broke his resolve, but he found his strength. "I'm going into Custer to talk to Rory. He owes me an explanation." He started toward his truck when he heard her angry reply.

"He was your partner and he betrayed you. Yet you'll give him a chance to explain. You won't extend the same courtesy to me. Fine."

Oh, dear me. I thought the fireworks were over. All four of the bad guys were rounded up and hauled off—and the fifth one died in the crash of Rupert Casper's SUV. The government got back the microchip listing the secret agents, Rory was saved, though a bit on the damaged side, and all the horses are okay. As a bonus, Rupert Casper has been charged with conspiracy to commit treason and a host of other things. That's the federal way—throw out two hundred charges knowing that at least some of them will stick. Suits me, as long as he ends up in jail for a long, long time.

So you would think Miss Cowgirl and Johnny Kreel would be in the house heating up the sheets in a major celebration.

Not a chance. Those two are letting a little bit of hurt get in the way of a whole lot of feeling good. Humanoids. They are the most inept creatures in the universe at clear communication of emotion. How did they manage to take over the planet? The two genders can't string two sentences together explaining their feelings without falling into the category of misleading, misconstrued or just plain misconceived.

I'm half-starved, sleep deprived, saddle sore and craving a tender trout fillet. But I have to put all my needs aside and deal with this foolishness or Johnny Kreel is liable to miss out on the best thing that ever crossed his path.

The one thing I've learned in this whole episode is that the horse has more sense than anyone else on this ranch. Black Jack, lead the way, son.

WATCHING JOHNNY DRIVE AWAY, Stephanie finally felt her temper ease. He'd made her mad enough to hog-tie him and hit him with a cattle prod—something she didn't approve of for any reason. But Johnny was willing to listen to Rory's explanations, yet he wouldn't even give her a chance. That was a low blow.

If the boot had been on the other foot, he would certainly have expected her to listen to him. In fact, when he'd finally confessed that he was at Running Horse Ranch on a pretext, she'd listened. And she'd forgiven him, because she could understand being caught between his desire to protect his country and his need to be honest.

Obviously, he could dish it out but he couldn't take it.

She stomped into the house, only to be met by a hissing Familiar.

"If he won't listen, there's nothing I can do," she said.

Familiar wrapped his arms around her lower leg in a bear hug and bit her shin.

"Hey!" She stepped out of his painful embrace. "What is it? You've got my attention."

Familiar ran to the table, jumped onto it. From there he leaped to the counter and finally snagged her truck keys off the hook on the wall. With great expertise, he hefted them at her.

They fell at her feet with a clang.

"Oh, no," she said, backing away from them. "I'm not chasing after Johnny Kreel and I certainly am not going to the hospital where Rory is being held."

Familiar sailed to the floor. He hooked the keys with a paw and dropped them on top of her foot. "Me-ow." It was a command, not a request.

Sighing, Stephanie scooped up the keys. Dammit, the cat was right. She couldn't let Johnny walk out of her life without giving it 100 percent. He might not listen, but he was damn sure going to hear what she had to say.

Familiar was already in the truck when she got there. The Feds had repaired both trucks and had also assured Stephanie that the barn would be rebuilt. This was all part of her agreement to keep silent about everything that had happened. She didn't view it as a payoff, only as a settlement.

She headed for Custer, wondering what her reception would be. She had no goodbyes to say to Rory. She was over her initial surge of anger, and now when she thought of him there was only a quiet numbness. Maybe in time it would wear off and she'd feel the pain that his actions had caused. For now, though, she was happy to leave it alone. There were more important things to attend to.

RORY LOOKED LIKE HELL, and Johnny couldn't say he didn't deserve it. The man had left devastation in his wake. Johnny couldn't suppress the sense of betrayal he felt, but he had come for answers, not recriminations. He wasn't prepared for the sense of sorrow he felt when Rory saw him and his face lit up.

"I didn't think you'd come," Rory said. Even though he struggled to breathe, one arm was handcuffed to the bed rail. He was a federal prisoner.

"I had some questions."

The smile fell from Rory's face. "I expect you do." He pointed to a chair.

"I'll stand, thank you," Johnny said. "Why, Rory? Why did you do this?"

"Which part? Taking the microchip or involving Stephanie?"

"Take your pick."

Rory closed his eyes, and Johnny could see the exhaustion and pain. "You won't believe it, but I didn't have a choice."

"You're right. I don't believe it."

"I had to get the microchip. The man who had it put it on the market to the highest bidder, who happened to be Carlos Diego. When he sent me to get it, I knew I couldn't let it fall into his hands, and I couldn't leave it with Capricorn, who'd already arranged to double-cross Carlos, retrieve the chip and sell it to a terrorist group. I had no choice. I had to take it, and I had to make it disappear. Until I could figure out a way to keep the agents on the list safe and to satisfy Carlos."

"And you thought taking it and disappearing as the victim of a plane crash would accomplish that? Why didn't you call me? Why didn't you contact Bevins or someone at Omega?"

"Carlos had begun to suspect me. It was a matter of days, maybe hours, before he ordered me killed. If I died on my own, I thought I could come back here, retrieve the microchip and turn it in. Then maybe the agency would give Stephanie some protection."

"You didn't think Carlos would figure out that you were alive?"

Rory bit his lip. "I covered my tracks pretty well."

"That's why we're all here in South Dakota. You left a long trail, Rory." Johnny felt his anger bloom again. "And Stephanie? What about her? You put her life in danger and she loves you."

"I love her, too," Rory said softly. "No one will ever believe it. Least of all her. But I do love her."

"Fine way to show it."

"I thought I could protect her," Rory said. "I never meant to leave the microchip there. I had to stay hidden longer than I expected. And then…"

Johnny cut him no slack. He waited.

"Then when I realized what I'd done and how badly it must have hurt her, I didn't want her to know I was alive. I thought I could get into the cabin, get the microchip and be gone. She'd never have to know my death was a lie."

Johnny threw his hands up. "So you're a coward on top of everything else."

Instead of the anger he expected from Rory, his old partner merely nodded his head. "As it turns out, that's exactly what I am."

"And yet she still loves you." Johnny paced the room. "I saw the two of you, the way you touched her cheek and the way she looked at you. Despite everything, she still loves you."

Awareness dawned in Rory's eyes. "So that's what's eating you. You've fallen for her."

Johnny gritted his teeth, but he didn't deny it. Rory's laughter made him want to throttle the man.

"You're a fool, Johnny. You can't see what's in front of you. The woman cares for you, not me."

Johnny stopped pacing. "What?"

"We were playing a strategy. She had to make me see the earring. We had to act like lovers. Carlos was going to kill us and Stephanie wanted me to know the microchip was safe, hanging from her ear. That way it didn't matter if Carlos's gunmen went to the cabin and tore it apart. There wasn't anything there for them to find."

Johnny processed everything Rory was saying, but he found it difficult to believe.

"Ask her," Rory said. "She loved me once, I think, but I destroyed that. Ask her."

Chapter Twenty

Stephanie thought her heart would drum out of her chest as she waited quietly at the hospital door, standing ajar, and listened to the conversation between Johnny and Rory.

Familiar, too, eavesdropped, nodding his head as Rory talked. When Rory urged Johnny to ask her about her feelings, Familiar surged through the door with a cry.

Startled, Johnny turned and faced her. She froze. For several seconds that felt like an eternity, they simply stared at each other. Then Johnny took two long steps toward her and she ran to meet him.

His arms wrapped around her and pulled her against his lean, hard body and she clung to him, never wanting to let go.

"I'm sorry," she said. "I never meant to hurt you."

"I should have seen that," he said. "I would have done the same thing."

When she looked over Johnny's shoulder, she saw Rory watching them. Sadness tinged his handsome features, but true to the man she'd first fallen for, he winked at her. "The best man won," he said.

She knew he was hiding his pain behind casual banter. She

eased out of Johnny's arms, but she kept her hand on his shoulder, kept the connection she wanted more than anything. "I heard, Rory. At least you didn't sell out your country."

"No, just my fiancée," he said. "I'll never be able to make up to you what I did. It won't fix things, but at least you know I recognize what I've lost. And I did remove the lead rope from that black stallion after Plenty let him loose. I remembered what you said about the danger of dangling ropes, so I unsnapped it."

She felt the trace of a smile touch her lips. "That was the right thing to do. Rory, I suspect you'll find someone else who makes you happy. You've got the gift of attracting people."

"No one like you, Stephanie. You're one in a million."

"I agree with you on that," Johnny said. He drew Stephanie against his side. "I'll call Bevins and explain all of this. Someone should remove the handcuffs."

"No worries," Rory said, jangling the cuffs merrily. "It's just a bit of bling."

Stephanie eased to the bed. "I'm sorry I shot you."

"It did put a kink in my plans," Rory admitted, "but I deserved a lot worse."

"Yeah, you did." She took the sting out with a smile. "I wish you the best, Rory."

"You've got a good man there, Stephanie. A better man than I'll ever be. And you deserve it. I'm sorry for everything that's happened."

Stephanie held out her hand to Johnny, and he grasped it. Things had turned out far better than she'd ever expected. Rory would straighten out the tangled mess of his involvement with Carlos Diego and the microchip. "What are you going to do, Rory?" she asked.

"Maybe start a charter airline down in sunny Florida. I mean the government gave me flying lessons. Seems like a shame to waste them. And I enjoy the life. And you?"

Stephanie didn't get a chance to answer. Johnny spoke up. "Build Running Horse Ranch into a training facility. Maybe start some classes on how to properly gentle a horse."

"That's a tough life for a woman alone," Rory said. "Somehow, though, I don't think she'll be by herself."

"Meow!" Familiar added from the foot of the bed.

ANOTHER CASE CLOSED. Another couple brought together by Familiar, Black Cat Detective. When I get too old to actively solve cases, maybe I should take up dispensing romantic advice in some kind of newspaper column. I could call it Familiar Wisdom. *It could be a smash success. If I could just teach humanoids to understand cat lingo, I could do talk radio.*

The potential is endless.

Until then, though, it's back to the ranch while I wait for Eleanor and Peter to show up and fetch me. And not a moment too soon. It's not that I don't care about Stephanie and Johnny, but I get the sense that they won't really miss me. At least not for a few months. They'll have Black Jack to watch over them and protect them. With Rupert Casper headed for prison, Stephanie is going to take in all of the horses at his place. They'll have a wonderful life now, and from what I heard, at least one of Casper's ranch hands is coming to Running Horse to work with Stephanie and Johnny as they build the ranch's reputation of a place to gentle horses.

So I'm heading back to D.C. and my Clotilde.

She's kept the home fires burning, and I'm ready for some

*of Eleanor's gourmet cooking, a pillow in front of the hearth
in the library and my calico delight to snuggle against.*
    Life is good.

* * * * *

RICK'S APPOINTMENT with his attorney early Wednesday morning went only moderately better than his meeting with social services the day before. The prognosis wasn't great—but at least his attorney was going to file a motion for DNA testing. Just so Rick could petition to see the child…his sister's baby. The sister he didn't know he had until it was too late.

The rest of what his attorney said had been downhill from there.

Cell phone in hand before he'd even reached his Nitro, Rick punched in the speed dial number he'd programmed the day before.

Maybe foster parent Sue Bookman hadn't received his message. Or had lost his number. Maybe she didn't want to talk to him. At this point he didn't much care what she wanted.

"Hello?" She answered before the first ring was complete. And sounded breathless.

Young and breathless.

"Ms. Bookman?"

"Yes. This is Rick Kraynick, right?"

"Yes, ma'am."

"I recognized your number on caller ID," she said, her

voice uneven, as though she was still engaged in whatever physical activity had her so breathless to begin with. "I'm sorry I didn't get back to you. I've been a little…distracted."

The words came in more disjointed spurts. Was she jogging?

"No problem," he said, when, in fact, he'd spent the better part of the night before watching his phone. And fretting. "Did I get you at a bad time?"

"No worse than usual," she said, adding, "Better than some. So, how can I help?"

God, if only this could be so easy. He'd ask. She'd help. And life could go well. At least for one little person in his family.

It would be a first.

"Mr. Kraynick?"

"Yes. Sorry. I was… Are you sure there isn't a better time to call?"

"I'm bouncing a baby, Mr. Kraynick. It's what I do."

"Is it Carrie?" he asked quickly, his pulse racing.

"How do you know Carrie?" She sounded defensive, which wouldn't do him any good.

"I'm her uncle," he explained, "her mother's— Christy's—older brother, and I know you have her."

"I can neither confirm nor deny your allegations, Mr. Kraynick. Please call social services." She rattled off the number.

"Wait!" he said, unable to hide his urgency. "Please," he said more calmly. "Just hear me out."

"How did you find me?"

"A friend of Christy's."

"I'm sorry I can't help you, Mr. Kraynick," she said softly. "This conversation is over."

"I grew up in foster care," he said, as though that gave him some special privilege. Some insider's edge.

"Then you know you shouldn't be calling me at all."

"Yes... But Carrie is my niece," he said. "I need to see her. To know that she's okay."

"You'll have to go through social services to arrange that."

"I'm sure you know it's not as easy as it sounds. I'm a single man with no real ties and I've no intention of petitioning for custody. They aren't real eager to give me the time of day. I never even knew Carrie's mother. For all intents and purposes, our mother didn't raise either one of us. All I have going for me is half a set of genes. My lawyer's on it, but it could be weeks—months—before this is sorted out. Carrie could be adopted by then. Which would be fine, great for her, but then I'd have lost my chance. I don't want to take her. I won't hurt her. I just have to see her."

"I'm sorry, Mr. Kraynick, but..."

* * * * *

*Find out if Rick Kraynick will ever have
a chance to meet his niece.
Look for A DAUGHTER'S TRUST
by Tara Taylor Quinn,
available in September 2009.*

We'll be spotlighting a different series
every month throughout 2009
to celebrate our 60th anniversary.

**Look for Harlequin® Superromance®
in September!**

*Celebrate with
The Diamond Legacy
miniseries!*

Follow the stories of four cousins as they come to terms
with the complications of love and what it means to
be a family. Discover with them the sixty-year-old secret
that rocks not one but two families.

A DAUGHTER'S TRUST by *Tara Taylor Quinn*
September

FOR THE LOVE OF FAMILY by *Kathleen O'Brien*
October

LIKE FATHER, LIKE SON by *Karina Bliss*
November

A MOTHER'S SECRET by *Janice Kay Johnson*
December

Available wherever books are sold.

REQUEST YOUR FREE BOOKS!

2 FREE NOVELS PLUS 2 FREE GIFTS!

HARLEQUIN®

INTRIGUE®

Breathtaking Romantic Suspense

YES! Please send me 2 FREE Harlequin Intrigue® novels and my 2 FREE gifts (gifts are worth about $10). After receiving them, if I don't wish to receive any more books, I can return the shipping statement marked "cancel." If I don't cancel, I will receive 6 brand-new novels every month and be billed just $4.24 per book in the U.S. or $4.99 per book in Canada. That's a savings of close to 15% off the cover price! It's quite a bargain! Shipping and handling is just 50¢ per book.* I understand that accepting the 2 free books and gifts places me under no obligation to buy anything. I can always return a shipment and cancel at any time. Even if I never buy another book from Harlequin, the two free books and gifts are mine to keep forever.

182 HDN EYTR 382 HDN EYT3

Name	(PLEASE PRINT)	
Address		Apt. #
City	State/Prov.	Zip/Postal Code

Signature (if under 18, a parent or guardian must sign)

Mail to the **Harlequin Reader Service:**
IN U.S.A.: P.O. Box 1867, Buffalo, NY 14240-1867
IN CANADA: P.O. Box 609, Fort Erie, Ontario L2A 5X3

Not valid to current subscribers of Harlequin Intrigue books.

**Are you a current subscriber of Harlequin Intrigue books
and want to receive the larger-print edition?
Call 1-800-873-8635 today!**

* Terms and prices subject to change without notice. Prices do not include applicable taxes. Sales tax applicable in N.Y. Canadian residents will be charged applicable provincial taxes and GST. Offer not valid in Quebec. This offer is limited to one order per household. All orders subject to approval. Credit or debit balances in a customer's account(s) may be offset by any other outstanding balance owed by or to the customer. Please allow 4 to 6 weeks for delivery. Offer available while quantities last.

Your Privacy: Harlequin is committed to protecting your privacy. Our Privacy Policy is available online at www.eHarlequin.com or upon request from the Reader Service. From time to time we make our lists of customers available to reputable third parties who may have a product or service of interest to you. If you would prefer we not share your name and address, please check here. ☐

HI09R

You're invited to join our Tell Harlequin Reader Panel!

By joining our new reader panel you will:

- Receive Harlequin® books—they are FREE and yours to keep with no obligation to purchase anything!
- Participate in fun online surveys
- Exchange opinions and ideas with women just like you
- Have a say in our new book ideas and help us publish the best in women's fiction

In addition, you will have a chance to win great prizes and receive special gifts!
See Web site for details. Some conditions apply.
Space is limited.

To join, visit us at

www.TellHarlequin.com.

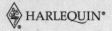
HARLEQUIN®

INTRIGUE®

COMING NEXT MONTH

Available September 8, 2009

www.eHarlequin.com

HICNMBPA0809